Laura Upside-Down

Laura
Upside-Down

a novel by
DORIS BUCHANAN SMITH

VIKING KESTREL

VIKING KESTREL

Viking Penguin Inc., 40 West 23rd Street, New York, New York 10010, U.S.A.
Penguin Books Ltd, Harmondsworth, Middlesex, England
Penguin Books Australia Ltd, Ringwood, Victoria, Australia
Penguin Books Canada Limited, 2801 John Street, Markham, Ontario, Canada L3R 1B4
Penguin Books (N.Z.) Ltd, 182–190 Wairau Road, Auckland 10, New Zealand

First Edition
Copyright © 1984 by Doris Buchanan Smith
First published in 1984 by Viking Penguin Inc.
Published simultaneously in Canada
Printed in U.S.A.
1   2   3   4   5   88   87   86   85   84

Library of Congress Cataloging in Publication Data
Smith, Doris Buchanan.   Laura upside-down.
Summary: Ten-year-old Laura must deal with her unease about her lack of
religious upbringing, when her best friends are Jewish and Christian, and with her
feelings for a mysterious neighbor who seems to be a witch.   I. Title.
PZ7.S64474Lau   1984   [Fic]   84-3689   ISBN 0-670-41998-2

For my mentor, Ruth Herbert,
small in stature, large in spirit.
Your absence leaves a huge hole.

And for Helyn Calibash,
wherever you are.

Contents

CONTENTS

Laura Upside-Down

Saints and Sinners

Quick as a cricket, Laura Catherine Frazier changed her position from upside-down to inside-out. Hands and feet against the pear tree limb, she stared goggle-eyed at her friend Anna, her chin at Anna's forehead, her forehead at Anna's chin.

"I wish I could do that, Laura Cat," Anna said.

"Well, you could if you tried," Laura said. She unwound herself and began again. "You never try anything, Anna." She thrust her hips, chest, and shoulders outward and down and popped into skinning-the-cat.

"I can't," Anna whispered.

"Of course you can," said Laura, her scraggly pink-blond

3

hair standing out from her head and her Hanover Hounds T-shirt drooping toward her chin. The warm south Georgia sun baked her arms, even in late October. She hated her own scrawny hair and bones and admired Anna's thickness of hair and bones. Anna's hair was long and hung straight and sure to the waist. Laura's hair wasn't sure about anything, especially what direction to go in. Anyone as sturdy as Anna could do anything, Laura thought.

"Laura Cat, I can't," Anna said, sounding urgent. "It's a sin."

"What?" Laura said. She righted herself and flung herself down from the tree. "Skinning-the-cat is a sin?" They didn't deal in sins in her family, though she'd heard plenty about sins from others. But she'd never heard of this one.

Anna whispered, but loudly, "No-o-o. It's pants. It's a sin for a girl to wear pants."

"What?" Laura said. She'd never heard of this one, either. "You mean you're not wearing pants?" This time she whispered, too.

Anna's dark-complexioned face turned burgundy. "This kind of pants," she whispered back, tugging on the sides of her skirt. "Outside pants. It's a sin for a girl to wear pants, the Bible says."

Laura almost said, "Oh, pooh," but Marm and Daddy wouldn't like it if she said that. They told her to respect other people's beliefs.

"Well, I've got to go," Anna said, all agitated and nervous. Anna never stayed around for a disagreement.

4

"Go, then!" Laura shouted after Anna, and she didn't even say, "Don't forget about tomorrow." For all she knew, Halloween parties were a sin, too. Hands on hips, she marched into the kitchen.

"Did you know Anna thinks I'm sinful?" she asked Daddy. "For all I know, the whole Banner family thinks I'm sinful."

"Hey, whoa, Sugarpuss. What brought all this on?" Daddy turned from the stove, where he was sautéing onions and peppers, and caught Laura up in a hug.

"I guess they've thought I was sinful since I was three," she said. "Ever since they first met me." She clearly remembered the dark green overalls she had treasured and worn to playschool when she was three. "For seven years they've thought I was sinful." She also remembered an infant picture of herself in a pale yellow jumpsuit with a hood. "They probably think I was born sinful."

"What brought all this on?" Daddy asked again, as he turned to stir the onions and peppers.

"Pants," she said, grasping the sides of her jeans as Anna had grasped her skirt. In spite of her upset, she took a deep whiff of the kitchen smells. Onions cooking was her favorite smell. "Can you believe Anna said it was a sin for a girl to wear pants?"

"Well, certainly, if you say she said it, I believe she said it."

"No wonder she never does anything adventurous. How can you be adventurous in a skirt?" She thought of the things she liked to do best: somersaults, handstands, headstands, cartwheels, tree climbing. "Where do people get such ideas?" She stomped her foot to shake off hurt feelings. How could one of your best friends think you were sinful and you not even know it?

"Well, now," Daddy said. "How long a discussion do you want?"

Laura sighed. He might begin with Adam and Eve. Marm said it took "all of history" for Daddy to explain anything. She didn't want that long a discussion.

Anna didn't forget about the Halloween party, and Marm kept her promise and stayed out of the kitchen while Laura, Anna, and Zipporah prepared refreshments.

One set of gingerbread men was baking while Laura and Anna lifted the second set to another cookie sheet. Twice Laura's gingerbread men tore, once an arm and once a leg. Anna transferred hers whole, without having to stop and patch any.

Zipporah made spiced cider, mixing cinnamon into apple juice. She was spindly-limbed like Laura but had dense dark hair like Anna's. Today Zipporah's hair was braided and coiled around her head.

"Mmmm," said Zipporah, licking the spoon she'd used to stir. "I could drink every bit of this cider. Everything smells so good."

"Drink water," Laura said, barely able to resist the tangy odors herself. What she liked best was that she and her friends were creating these delectable aromas themselves. Always

6

before, even if she was helping, it was Marm or Daddy who made the kitchen smell delicious.

When every last gingerbread man lay cooling on the table, Laura decided they should each have one, along with a cup of cider. "After all," she said, "it's our party." She bit into the toe of her ginger man and nibbled slowly, letting the spicy sweetness linger on her tongue.

Besides the three of them, there were five friends coming to the party, Karen, Pam, Renee, Susan, and Tammy. Or, as Zipporah quipped, K, P, and R, S, T. Originally they had wanted a huge party. Then they had decided they wanted to do it by themselves instead of having their mothers prepare everything, and the more they thought about it, the smaller the party got. They were each going to be in charge of one game. Anna was making a Pin the Grin on the Pumpkin game and had an orange bandanna for a blindfold. Zipporah was keeping her game a secret, but said it had to be first. Laura was doing charades, though Zipporah had protested that it wasn't a Halloween game. "If I use mysteries and scary things for titles, it will be a Halloween game," Laura had said.

In the den they began to make decorations. Laura took sheet after sheet of construction paper and cut out Halloween cats and witches and jack-o'-lanterns. Zipporah cut and pasted and joined narrow orange-and-black strips until she had nearly disappeared beneath a mound of paper chain.

"That's all you've done, Zipporah?" Laura said, glancing at her own stack of cutouts, which actually seemed much smaller than the garlands of paper chain

"It's miles and miles," Zipporah said, taking hold of one end, stepping out of the accumulation, and trailing it around the room.

"Yeah, Laura Cat," Anna said. "It's enough." Anna was folding strips of paper back and forth to make accordion legs for a cat. "Why are you grouchy about Zipporah's paper chain?"

Laura glared at Anna. Had Anna forgotten that only yesterday she'd called Laura sinful? Well, I'm sinful today, too, she thought, looking at her jeans. And Zipporah is sinful, too. Only Anna was wearing a skirt. But Laura knew she had grouched at Zipporah because she hadn't grouched at Anna. In the seven years the three of them had known one another, Laura had seldom had a squabble with Anna, whereas she and Zipporah often fussed and made up. Dad called her friendship with Zipporah a rubber-band friendship. Mother called it stubborn and hardheaded. At least Zipporah knew how to take a grouch.

Marm peeked into the den. When Laura was a baby, Daddy affectionately called her Mother "My Arm," and when she was learning to talk, Laura turned the nickname into "Marm," which is what her brothers, Mark and Alex, called their mother, too. Marm had told Daddy that she wasn't his arm, so he never said it anymore, but he sometimes teased her and called her "My Leg" or "My Nose" or "My Ear."

"The gingerbread men looked wonderful," Marm said. "May I have a preview of the decorations?"

The girls looked at one another and nodded.

"I know you have your party all planned," Marm said when she'd finished admiring the decorations, "but I have a request to make."

The girls looked at one another again, then at Laura's mother.

"Just before dark," Marm said, "I'd like you and your guests to go over to Mrs. Large's for trick or treat."

"Trick or treat?" Laura said, looking at her mother in surprise. Trick-or-treating was history, something people used to do, going out on Halloween to knock on doors. When someone came to the door you stood there and said, "Trick or treat." They were supposed to give you a treat or else you would play a trick on them. Then somebody did something terrible, like poisoning some candy and putting razor blades in apples, and trick-or-treating was stopped. And Marm was asking them to do this? Laura shuddered.

"It's not really to Mrs. Large's but to the upstairs apartment." Laura knew where—up the outside stairs of Mrs. Large's house. Another Laura, a girl who used to baby-sit for them, had just moved away. Laura was sorry that the other Laura had moved. She had liked her a lot, and now they'd have to start over with a new baby-sitter, and Laura thought she was getting too old for that. Mark and Alex were seven and three and still needed one, but Marm and Daddy said Laura was too young for the responsibility.

"There's a woman who has just moved in," Marm continued. "She's been away for a long time, and she doesn't know that children don't go trick-or-treating anymore, and she has spent all morning making popcorn balls to give away.''

"With razor blades?" Laura asked.

"Oh, Laura Cat," Zipporah said. "Don't be silly. My mother said that only happened once or twice. It didn't actually happen sixteen thousand times like everyone thinks. Isn't that right, Mrs. Frazier?''

Marm confirmed Zipporah's statement. "A shame, too,'' she added. "Such a fun custom. We used to have such a grand time.''

Laura shrugged. It sounded like a rude custom to her, to knock on someone's door and ask for a treat.

"And with the poisoned candy it was even the children's own father who did it,'' Zipporah said. "For the insurance money. Isn't that right, Mrs. Frazier?''

Marm again confirmed Zipporah's statement, but she did not add to it. Laura thought that if they were going to have a game of telling horror stories, Zipporah would certainly win.

"What is she going to do with all those popcorn balls?'' Marm asked. "You could make it a part of your party.''

"Hey, that's a good idea,'' said Anna. "If she has lots and lots, we can change masks and go back.''

"That sounds greedy,'' Zipporah said.

"I wasn't thinking greedy,'' Anna said. "I was thinking kind, not to leave her with all those popcorn balls when she expects to give them away.''

"Okay,'' Laura said to Marm. "Okay?'' She looked at Anna and Zipporah. After all, it was their party, too. They both said okay.

10

When the decorations were finished, they began putting them around. With tape and a ladder, they strung the paper chain from doors to windows and even back and forth through the enameled yellow chandelier.

"Balloons," Zipporah said, waving a bag of orange and black balloons.

"I have to go," Anna said.

"Not until you blow your share," Zipporah said, ripping open the bag and starting with an orange one. "Do at least five," she told Anna, her own breath already expanding the balloon.

Anna took a black balloon and started blowing. Her cheeks puffed out but the balloon did not. Laura had already blown one up but was struggling in vain to pull the end of the balloon around her slender fingers and into a knot.

"You're both helpless," Zipporah said, deftly tying her first balloon and taking a second and stretching it sideways. "Stretch it first." She blew and knotted her second balloon, then took Laura's and knotted it, too.

"I can tie them," Anna said. "I just can't get them blown up." So Laura blew and Anna tied and Zipporah kept ahead of them both. But by the time Anna and Zipporah had gone home for supper and to change into their costumes, the den looked wonderfully, wickedly Halloween.

Wonderfully, Wickedly Halloween

At supper Laura said, "With all the witches and goblins and such, wouldn't you think Halloween would be sinful?" She was still plagued by Anna's remark.

"What does 'sinful' mean?" Mark asked.

"Witches and goblins," Alex said. He had climbed on the furniture and broken the paper chain twice already, touching it as he named the colors.

"We'll get to 'sinful' later," Daddy said to seven-year-old Mark. And to Laura he said, "Quite the opposite of sinful, Halloween was originally a religious holiday."

"A religious holiday!" Laura exclaimed.

"Tomorrow is All Saints' Day," Marm said. "It's also called All Hallows' Day."

" 'To hallow' means to honor something or someone as holy," Daddy said.

"Such as saints," Marm added. "And the night before All Hallows' Day is All Hallow Evening."

"All Hallow E'en," Daddy said.

"Halloween," Mark said, pleased to have kept track of the conversation.

"Then how did witches get attached to it?" asked Laura.

"Witches ride brooms," said Alex.

"What are saints?" Mark asked.

"This is only the dinner hour," Daddy said.

"Yeah, Mark," Laura said. "We don't have time for all of history."

"Witches tonight, since it's Halloween. Saints and sinners later. Okay, Mark?" Daddy reached for paper and pencil, wrote "saints and sinners," leaned toward the buffet, and dropped the paper into a blue ceramic jug.

Mark folded his arms and grumped. "I already have sixteen questions in that jar."

Marm reached over and touched Mark's hair. "I know," she said. "You're such a question box."

"But I want to know," he said.

"Well, so do I," Daddy said. "I want to know about witches. What can you tell me about witches?"

"They wear pointy hats," Mark said.

"They're bad," said Alex.

"But how come they are connected with Halloween if Halloween is a religious holiday?" Laura said, trying to keep Daddy on track. He always went four ways at once with any topic.

"Do you know the saying 'Beauty is in the eye of the beholder'?"

Laura sighed. There he goes, she thought.

"I don't," Mark said, moving right along in Daddy's direction. "What does it mean?"

"Well, your mother happens to think I'm handsome, but someone else might not think so. It depends on the eye of whoever is doing the looking."

"I look at Laura Cat," Alex said. He nodded his head vigorously. "She's handsome."

"And you're a sweetie," Laura said to Alex. She knew that Daddy would take his own good time to explain why witches were attached to a holy day.

"I get it," Mark said. "Like Haim loves that ugly old pinscher dog of his."

"Affenpinscher," Laura said. "Think of a fishy dog. A fish's fin and a sister's pinch." She reached over and tweaked Mark's ear.

"Owwww!" he howled and smacked at her hand.

Haim was Zipporah's little brother. Like Mark, he was seven years old. And the affenpinscher was, Laura agreed, a silly-looking little dog.

"It's the same with witches," Dad said. "Witches are

14

considered evil, but evil is sometimes in the eye of the beholder.''

"I get it," Laura said. "Like wearing pants."

"I get it, too," Alex said. "Laura Cat is in my eye." He looked around, quite pleased with himself when they all laughed.

The doorbell rang and Laura jumped up. "That's Anna and Zipporah already," she said. All of a sudden everything was rushed. She had to get into her costume, and she still hadn't found out why witches are connected with Halloween.

"I don't even have my costume on!" Laura said as she opened the door for her friends. They hadn't told each other what they'd be dressed as, so Laura was surprised. Zipporah was a sleek black cat in leotards and tights, with eared cap, whiskers, and a long, braided yarn tail.

"Oh, Zipporah, that looks great," she said. "And Anna, you're beautiful. How did you ever think of that?" The girls came in, and Anna, whose face was behind a mask of the full moon, shrugged. The moon was yellow with a face in it, and Anna wore a long, dark blue dress with iridescent stars pinned here and there on the skirt.

"I didn't want anything scary," Anna said. "I hate to be scared."

Anna and Zipporah followed Laura to Laura's bedroom, where she put on a strange combination of gaudy clothes and jewelry.

"Are you going to be a Gypsy, Laura Cat?" Anna asked.

"A Gypsy princess," Laura said as she stared at herself in the mirror and darkened her eyebrows. She drew thick strokes of crimson onto her lips, and just as she was dotting her cheeks with rouge, the doorbell rang again. The cat, the full moon, and the Gypsy princess ran to the door.

Dracula and a ghost were there.

"Who is it? Who is it?" the three hostesses asked the guests. "Is it Karen and Tammy?" It was. And Renee, Susan, and Pam soon showed up as a monster, a witch, and a pumpkin.

"We're all here, and we're all something different, and my game is first," Zipporah said.

"My I interrupt with a suggestion?" Marm asked, coming in and complimenting every costume before she went on. "Would you mind terribly if your game was second?" she asked Zipporah. "Since it's already getting dark, why don't you do the trick-or-treating first? And is it all right if Mark and Alex go along? Daddy will walk you to the corner."

Laura shrugged but Zipporah and Anna quickly said, "Sure."

"Would you like to explain the situation to your guests, or shall I?" Marm asked.

"You," Laura said quickly. It would sound strange enough coming from her mother, Laura thought. She herself would probably mix it up and make it worse.

Marm told about the woman who had been away and how she'd spent the afternoon making popcorn balls.

"Where has she been?" asked Pam the pumpkin. The question startled Laura because she hadn't thought to ask.

"Why don't we just have her send over the popcorn balls?" asked Karen Dracula.

Laura really liked Karen's idea but knew the point was to have ghosts and goblins go to the door of the popcorn-ball maker.

"Try to see how many she has," Anna said as Daddy walked them to the corner. "Then we'll know how many times to go back."

Laura and Zipporah started out first, with Alex. They crossed the street, walked to the second house, and followed a path around to the side steps, which were steep and dark. A candle glowed at the top of the stairs. Without any hesitation, Zipporah moved right up the stairs.

"Come on, Laura Cat," Alex said, tugging on her hand when she hung back.

At the top of the stairs, Zipporah was already knocking on the door. Laura started up with Alex, feeling embarrassed. What if there was no one ready for the trick-or-treaters or no popcorn balls?

A witch opened the door, and Laura grinned and stepped right up. The woman was ready for them, and even in costume. Ooooh, so witchy, Laura thought. Long gray hair straggled past her shoulders and her face was haggard in the candlelight. From inside the apartment candles glowed from everywhere, orange light flickering shadows across furniture and walls.

"Trick or treat," Zipporah said. Laura had forgotten to say it. The witch gazed at them intently, examining their costumes, examining them. Then she handed them each a wax-paper-wrapped popcorn ball. Laura shivered and suddenly believed in poisoned popcorn balls.

"Thank you," she said, at least remembering to say that.

"Thank you," said Alex. He pulled down his ghost mask to look at the popcorn ball and the witch. Zipporah said thanks, too, and the girls barely managed to reach the bottom of the stairs before they started giggling.

"Did you see all the candles?" Laura asked, as though anyone who'd been to the top of the stairs could have missed seeing them.

"She was so spooky," Zipporah said. "This is fun!" They looked up as they walked away, and saw a lighted candle in every upstairs window.

"How many popcorn balls?" Anna asked when they met Daddy and the others at the corner. Karen, Tammy, and Mark immediately started across the street for their turn.

"I forgot to look," Laura said. "She was dressed like a witch. Neat. Creepy."

"Dozens," said Zipporah. "I say we go three times each, and that's enough, even if she has a hundred popcorn balls."

When the second group returned, Renee, Susan, and Pam set out, and Zipporah and Laura changed masks with Tammy and Karen.

"You look funny," Anna said. Zipporah had become a ghost cat and Laura had become Mrs. Gypsy Dracula.

When Laura, Zipporah, and Mark were ready for their second turn, Laura noticed Anna. "The full moon in the sky has

18

not gone trick-or-treating," she said, grabbing Anna by the hand. Zipporah, with Mark, was already off down the sidewalk. "You have to do this," Laura said, bracing herself to tug at Anna's hand. She was surprised at Anna's strength. How could someone who never turned upside-down be so strong? she wondered.

"I don't have to if I don't want to—do I, Mr. Frazier?"

"No, you certainly don't," Daddy said. "There are some things in this life that we have to do whether we want to or not, but this is not one of them."

Still pulling on Anna, Laura frowned. Daddy couldn't just say anything without adding to it.

"I *will* go," Anna said, snatching herself loose from Laura's grip, "but not because you're trying to make me." Anna followed Laura, who followed Zipporah and Mark. Laura's former reluctance was shed in the face of Anna's.

"Come on," she said to Anna, as Alex had said to her.

"I don't like to be scared," Anna said, stopping halfway up the stairs, clinging to the railing, refusing to move one step higher.

"She's only a witch, Anna," Laura said, joining Zipporah and Mark at the top.

"Haven't I seen that costume before?" the witch woman asked Laura. "I've never seen Dracula with jewelry, and I don't give out twice. There are too many children yet to come."

"It's Mrs. Dracula," Zipporah said.

Laura's mouth fell open behind the Dracula mask as she

held out a bedangled hand for a popcorn ball. How could Zipporah think so fast? She was tempted to add, "We didn't want to come get these popcorn balls in the first place, lady."

"May I have one for my friend?" Zipporah asked, indicating Anna, who was cowering on the stairs. "She's shy."

"Shy doesn't get a treat," the witch said, holding out a popcorn ball to coax Anna up the stairs. "Come on up. You have to take it yourself. Don't be afraid. I don't eat children for Halloween. Only for Thanksgiving." The witch took her eyes off Anna and looked at Mark. "Especially plump little boys. What a feast."

Mark whooped with the scary pleasure of it, and Anna fled without a popcorn ball. The woman's laugh sounded like a cackle.

"Ooooh!" Laura said, and grabbing Mark's hand, she dragged him down the stairs with her. "She's the best witch I've ever seen," she said, when they caught up with Anna.

"You'll never get me up there again," Anna said. "I don't like to be scared, especially in the dark."

"She didn't scare me," Mark said. "I'll eat *her* for Thanksgiving."

"Oh, Mark, yuck," Laura said. As Marm often said, there was such a thing as carrying things too far.

On the corner the others wer jabbering about the witch.

"Such realistic makeup," said Susan, who was wearing the witch mask.

"But did you notice?" Zipporah said. "I don't think she has on any makeup. I think that's really her own face."

20

"Ooooh," Laura said, as she put on Pam's pumpkin mask. "I mean it," Zipporah said. "You look carefully. I don't think she's made up at all. I think she really is an old hag."

No amount of persuasion could move Anna from Daddy and the streetlight on the corner when Zipporah and Laura set out again, for their third and last turn. When the witch opened the door, Laura looked carefully. She was not wearing makeup. She was really an old hag, as Zipporah had said.

When the witch saw Laura she stared and said, "There are those jewels again."

"It's the Pumpkin Princess," Zipporah said. Laura wondered why the witch woman was enchanted with the jewels and didn't notice anything peculiar about a ghost cat or a monster cat. "Don't you know the story of the Pumpkin Princess?" Zipporah asked.

Candles wavered from everywhere, and Laura steeled her nerves to keep looking at the witch when she handed out popcorn balls.

"No, I don't believe I know that story," the witch said. "Is it new?"

"Very new," Zipporah said.

Laura took her third popcorn ball and scurried down the stairs without saying thanks. They passed the next group in the yard.

"I don't think they should have gone," Laura whispered to Daddy when she was back on the corner. "I don't think anyone else should go."

"You will be the last," he said, sending off the next bunch

before the other group was back. "If she has any more pop-corn balls she'll have to eat them herself."

"But Daddy, I think she's a real witch." Laura stared into the dark, watching the figures of her friends reach the top of the stairs. The porch door opened, then the figures retreated. No one was snatched inside to be baked in an oven. Still, Laura took her breaths in huge gulps, holding each breath as long as possible. She was quite swimmy-headed by the time the last three were safely back on the corner. With Daddy, Mark, Alex, and twenty-seven popcorn balls, the party pals returned to Laura's house.

At last Zipporah announced her great secret "game." It was to be a pumpkin-carving contest. "Put the insides in this washtub," Zipporah said as she gave out pumpkins and par-ing knives. "Be careful," she added. "I don't know first aid."

"I do," said Renee the monster. "But be careful any-way."

"How did you get all this stuff over here?" Laura asked, though she recognized two of the knives.

"I have my ways," Zipporah said, then she continued tell-ing about her game. "There will be a prize for the best jack-o'-lantern, and a candle for each one. Then we'll use them for decorations." Zipporah turned to Anna and Laura. "That's why this game had to be first."

"I don't know how to carve it," Tammy said.

"Me, either," said Karen.

Zipporah explained how to cut out the top and hollow out

the inside by removing the seeds. Already the guts of pumpkins were splatting into the washtub.

"Oooh," Laura said, not about witches this time but at the contents of the washtub.

"It's like cantaloupe," Renee said.

"I hate cantaloupe," Pam said.

Laura, who'd gutted pumpkins before, was quickly ready to cut out eyes, nose, and mouth. She stood back and looked at the pumpkin to consider what sort of jack-o'-lantern it should become. She decided to make it a merry, twinkling one with stars for eyes. She slid the knife blade through the flesh of the pumpkin, and with ten slits of the knife she had one star-eye. When she stood back to admire it, she saw that the star was lopsided, but that looked even better, she thought, than a perfect star would have. She carved the second eye, then a circle for the nose and a toothless quarter-moon for the mouth. In a last burst of inspiration she draped some of her beads around the pumpkin head.

"Hey, great, Laura Cat," Zipporah said. "Look, everyone, it's the Pumpkin Princess."

"Hey," said Pam. "Sun, moon, and stars. Anna should have carved that pumpkin."

Now they all looked to see what kind of pumpkin Anna had made. The top, sides, and back of Anna's pumpkin were covered with cotton balls.

"What is it?" Laura asked.

"George Washington Pumpkin," Anna said. Everyone shrieked with delight, and Anna won the prize. Zipporah, who had carved a pumpkin herself, had them place two in each of the four den windows. Squat candles were set inside each one and lighted. The eight pumpkins grinned into the party room.

"What a wonderful surprise," Laura said to Zipporah. The party was off to a great start.

For charades, the group divided into two teams of four girls each, and the members of each team wrote the titles of mysteries on pieces of paper. By turns they each drew a title from the other team to act out for their own team to guess. Laura drew *The Mystery of the Flying Orange Pumpkin.*

"Oh, come on," she said, waving the slip at her opponents. "Who made this up?" *The Mystery of the Flying Orange Pumpkin,* indeed, she thought. "The same person who made up the Pumpkin Princess, I'll bet," she said, flapping the title in Zipporah's face.

"It's a real book," Zipporah said. "Haim has it. Mark gave it to him for his birthday. Ask your mother."

"Go ahead and play the game," Karen said.

By now everyone knew the imitation of Sherlock Holmes, so as soon as Laura hunched over and pretended to be looking through a magnifying glass for clues, everyone shouted, "Mystery!" That part was easy. Then she flapped her arms, and Pam quickly guessed "Flying." After that, Pam, Anna, and Renee jumped and jabbered their way into guessing "The Flying . . . *everything,*" without paying attention to what Laura was doing. They guessed bats, cats, turtles, and even "The Flying Paper Chain" when Laura pointed to it while pointing to everything orange in the room. Then she indicated blue things, black things, green things, yellow things, and vigorously shook her head. Then she returned to touching orange things and nodded until she thought her Gypsy princess head would nod right off her bejeweled shoulders.

At last someone shouted, "Orange!" and the other two knew immediately that it was the right word and wasted precious seconds joining the shout: "Orange! Orange!" With the jack-o'-lanterns in the windows, "Pumpkin" was easy, and finally they had it: *The Mystery of the Flying Orange Pumpkin*.

"Who made that up?" Renee asked.

For Pin the Grin, Anna took charge with her orange bandanna.

Someone had to say it, and this time it was Tammy. "Anna bandanna." Everyone groaned.

Laura was at an advantage in this game because she had a good sense of direction and even twirling didn't mix her up. She won Pin the Tail on the Donkey every time she played it. And this time it was her house. But her team had won charades and it wouldn't be right for her to win again. Anna tied the bandanna, blindfolding Laura, and then turned her. Laura purposely came out of the spin at the wrong angle and with total self-assuredness she guided the pin-with-the-grin directly into the wall. Her friends hooted with glee and she acted embarrassed. Other grins wound up as eyes, ears, or jagged decorations on the wall. Zipporah's grin came closest, so Zipporah won that prize.

Flushed with pleasure, Laura thought, We all won! She supposed it wasn't polite for the hostesses to win, but it was their very first party and it seemed exactly right.

They trooped into the dining room for refreshments. There was cider, candy corn, and popcorn balls; none of the gingerbread men had run away.

"What are we going to do with all these popcorn balls?" Karen asked.

"Get sick," Zipporah answered.

But when the party was over, everything had been consumed. The cider jugs were empty, and there was not one kernel of candy corn left over. The gingerbread men had run away only into stomachs, and even the popcorn balls—all twenty-seven—were gone. And no one got sick.

A Witch in the Rocking Chair

As a warning of the coming winter, the gold-and-blue October days turned into gray drizzle for November. Laura loved it. The day after the party, Laura's curiosity about Halloween's being a holy day had taken her to the *H* volume of the encyclopedia on the bookshelf. Halloween, before it was Halloween as we celebrate it, had been a Celtic harvest festival. Gifts were given to the evil spirits to keep them full and satisfied, so they would leave people alone during the coming winter. She was delighted to learn this early beginning of "trick or treat," and pleased that the climate in her part of the world had changed on schedule.

The following Monday morning, as Laura stepped off the

porch to go to school, Mark darted ahead. She tucked her books beneath her green-and-yellow raincape and slid her arms through the side slots to hold the books and keep them dry. In fifth grade they had a lot of books to carry and she could not run free, like Mark.

She was supposed to walk with Mark, but how could she? He was always running ahead or dawdling behind. When she complained to Marm, Marm said, "Well, just keep an eye out." This morning, while her eye was out, Mark disappeared around the corner.

When she reached the corner herself, she looked across the street and up at the witch's apartment. There was no eerie glow, nothing at all witchy about the sheer white curtains that hung at the window. The curtains didn't even look ghostly.

Zipporah, who lived across from the witch, stood at the end of the sidewalk to her house, waiting. Mark and Haim ran ahead, stomping through puddles they'd been told to avoid.

"Ma-ark!" Laura called, to caution and remind.

"I have my rainboots," he called. Laura shrugged; she was trying to be responsible. That was part of growing up—paying attention to things you didn't even notice when you were a little kid.

"She burned candles last night, too," Zipporah said, glancing over at the witch's apartment as they started toward school.

"Really?" Laura looked carefully but could see no signs of candle stubs on the windowsills. "Why, I wonder."

"I guess she's a real witch."

On the next corner, but across the street and on the same side as the witch's apartment, they met Anna. She ran out of her house to meet them, then turned to wave at two little faces in the window.

"They're so cute," Anna said of her toddler twin sisters. They were indeed, Laura agreed, but just let Anna wait until they were seven and splashing in puddles when she was supposed to be keeping an eye out!

At school, Laura was more excited about "after Halloween" than she'd ever been about "after Christmas," when everyone returned asking, "What did you get? What did you get?" When she chattered and asked her classmates what they'd done for Halloween, they gave dull, one-sentence responses.

"Our church had a carnival," one said.

"We bobbed for apples," said another.

She knew she couldn't brag about her own party, especially to people who hadn't been invited, and it was disappointing. She guessed Halloween didn't linger like Christmas. When Halloween was over, it was over.

At lunch period there was quiet excitement. Today was the first day of a new experiment they'd been preparing for since the first of school. Mr. Norris, the new school principal, had said he didn't know any reason that children old enough to be in school couldn't get themselves to the cafeteria on their own and sit where they chose. "When I was in elementary school," he said, "I hated lines."

Laura hadn't even known she hated lines until he said it, until there was the possibility of not having lines. The two months of hearing about it and getting used to the idea had seemed very long.

"Everything's so quiet," Anna whispered as she set her tray on the table beside Laura's and across from Zipporah's. Laura noticed they had all set their trays down without a *clunk*.

"Yeah," Laura said. "Everyone wants this to work."

"Do you realize this is the first time we've had school lunch together?" Zipporah asked.

Almost in unison they put napkins on their laps and popped open their cartons of milk and inserted straws.

"It's like another party," Anna said. "I hope it works. I like having lunch with both of you."

"Our party was so-o-o much fun," Laura said, leaning toward Anna and Zipporah so no one else would hear, so it wouldn't be boasting. It was good to be able to talk about it at last.

"Let's have another one," Anna said.

"Okay. When?" said Zipporah.

"What's the next holiday?" Laura asked. "Thanksgiving?"

"Yes, let's have a Thanksgiving party," Anna said. "At my house."

"Whoever heard of a Thanksgiving party?" Zipporah asked.

"This can be the first," Anna said. "I like that. There won't be anything scary."

After school, just as they were approaching Anna's corner, the two-day drizzle turned into hard, plump drops. The girls bolted onto Anna's porch, which, like the house, stood perched at an angle to the street. Laura looked down the street, trying to spot Mark. He was out of sight, but she didn't know whether he'd been washed away by the rain or whether he was at Haim's or already around the corner, at home.

"Oh, goody," Zipporah said. "We'll get to see the twins."

"How many times do I have to tell you not to call them twins?" Anna said. She took off her raincoat, shook it, and hung it over the porch swing.

"Well, that's what they are, aren't they?" Zipporah asked, repeating Anna's motions with her own raincoat, then stooping to pull off her boots.

"They are two individual little people. Everyone knows how I feel about that, Zip."

"Okay, okay," Zipporah said, raising her hands in surrender from her stooped position. Everyone also knew how Zipporah felt about being called "Zip."

"I wish I could be a twin," Laura said. "It would be fun." Sometimes she and Zipporah wore the same color clothes to school, like almost-twins. The school had Hanover Hounds T-shirts, and Friday was the day for wearing school shirts. Laura and Zipporah almost always did, but not Anna, never Anna. Laura added her raincoat to the collection and glanced at the drops of water gathering beneath the swing.

"I'd hate being a twin," Anna said. She mimicked things people said about them. " 'Two peas in a pod.' 'Aren't they adorable?' 'Just alike.' 'How do you ever tell them apart?' "

In the kitchen, two tiny look-alike toddlers stood up from

the midst of a clutter of toys. "Annan, Annan," they called, walking to their sister on stubby legs. She hugged them and they hugged her. One copying the other, they pointed to Laura and Zipporah, giggled, and hid their faces in Anna's skirt.

"Hello, Betsy," Zipporah said. "Hello, Bonnie."

Laura looked at Zipporah to see whether Zipporah really knew which twin was which. Laura certainly didn't, though she'd never tell Anna. The only thing that saved her was the fact that they were never dressed alike, so each time she saw them she found out which one was wearing which clothes and remembered it for that time.

"Hello, Laura. Hello, Zipporah," Mrs. Banner said from where she was mixing something at the counter. "You, too, Anna."

"Mama, can we have a Thanksgiving party here?" Anna asked.

"Whoever heard of a Thanksgiving party?" Mrs. Banner said, beat-beat-beating something in a bowl.

"We'll have the first one," Anna said.

Laura sat on the floor and began stacking the babies' blocks.

"You've just had a party, Anna," Mrs. Banner said, looking around at Laura and Zipporah. She slid the bowl off the counter and clasped it to her belly for a better angle at the beating. "I hear it was a lovely, fun party."

"But here," Anna said. "I want to have one here."

Laura concentrated on the blocks. Legs out in front of her, she had just become aware of her jeans, aware that she was in the Banners' house in jeans. She tucked her legs beneath her and wondered if Mrs. Banner thought parties were sinful, too.

"I loved the Halloween party, and I want to have a party here. I want to grow up to be a party-giver." Anna looked around at everyone as though, Laura thought, it was the world's most important announcement.

"Well, Anna—" Mrs. Banner began.

"I don't think that's anything you can be," Zipporah put in.

One of the toddlers, Betsy or Bonnie, took a swipe at Laura's block tower and sent it flying.

"Betsy, that's not very nice," Mrs. Banner said.

Ah, it's Betsy, Laura thought. She has on the blue. She glanced at Bonnie, who had on tan and yellow. Their clothes were alike, she noted, but different colors.

"Oh, that's all right," Laura said. "That's what babies like to do with blocks." To prove it, she restacked the blocks and Betsy scattered them again, and Laura stacked and Bonnie toppled. Laura built towers with both hands, and both girls giggled and pushed them down. Laura smiled up at Mrs. Banner, surprised that the woman didn't know that this is what babies did with blocks. Laura knew from Mark and Alex that real building would come when they were older. Besides, she thought, what do babies know about what's nice and what's not nice? Sometimes she wasn't so sure herself.

"Wel-l-l?" Anna said to her mother.

"We'll see," Mrs. Banner said, and Anna jumped with excitement.

33

We'll see, Laura thought. She hated "we'll see's."

"What's all the racket?" Mr. Banner asked, as he came into the kitchen. "Oh," he said when he saw the wreckage of block towers. "I didn't think you were beating that hard." He stepped to Anna's mother and kissed her cheek, then leaned over and kissed Anna.

Anna ringed his neck with her arms. "We're going to have a Thanksgiving party," she said. "Here."

Laura saw him look at Mrs. Banner, who raised her eyebrows. "Is that a fact?" he asked Anna, and that sounded worse to Laura than "We'll see." Even if she didn't like his words, she did like his striped overalls with all the pockets. His job was building houses, and unless he had a house closed in enough to work inside, he didn't work on rainy days. He had spent all the years Laura had known Anna turning this huge old Victorian house back into the showplace it had once been.

His presence doubled Laura's self-consciousness about her jeans. And she felt so small sitting here below them on the floor. She stood up, and when Zipporah looked her way, tugged on her jeans as a signal about her feelings. Zipporah was wearing jeans, too, but didn't seem bothered about it. Then Laura realized she had not told Zipporah what Anna had said about pants.

"What do you make when you cook?" Laura asked Mr. Banner, trying to cover her awkwardness with conversation.

"Me?" He laughed and ruffled Laura's wispy hair. "That's woman's work, Blondie."

34

"What's 'woman's work'?" Laura asked.

Mr. Banner shook his head and laughed lightly. He exchanged looks with Mrs. Banner, but didn't answer Laura's question.

"Cooking," Anna said. "Cooking, washing clothes, and housework is woman's work. Everyone knows that, Laura Cat."

I don't, Laura thought. She leaned over and built yet another block tower.

When she popped into her own house, after removing the dripping rain clothes one more time, she was jolted to see the witch right there in her living room. There was no one else in sight, just the witch sitting in the rocking chair, rocking, rocking. The woman's damp hair dripped rainwater onto the sides of a dark green blouse, turning it almost black.

"What are you doing here?" Laura asked.

"Rocking," the witch said.

Laura let her books fall in a *clunk* and ran from the room, calling for Marm. Down the hall, through the den, into the kitchen. "Marm, Marm, Marmy!"

"Here, Laura Cat, on the back porch," Marm called. They collided in the doorway.

"Marm, Marm," Laura said, pointing toward the living room, pointing, pointing, all words but "Marm" having left her.

"What is it, Laura Cat?" Glue brush in hand, Marm looked toward the living room, then back to the book she was rebinding. Mark and Alex were playing Chutes and Ladders on the porch floor.

Laura jabbed the hall air as though trying to make dents in it. "She—she—did you know she was here?"

"Who?" Marm said. She put the brush in the glue pot, then pushed past Laura and took long steps down the wide hall.

"The witch," Laura whispered to her mother's back. "The witch."

Marm reached the living room, saw whom Laura meant, and said, "Well, hello. May I help you with something?"

"I'm just rocking," the witch said.

In the hall, Laura clutched herself and bent over in pain. That woman was in their house and Marm hadn't even known it. She darted into the living room, crossed to the door, and locked it. Then she turned to stare at the witch and realized she'd just locked the witch *in*. She unlocked the door and opened it as far as it would go, willing the witch to leave.

"I'm Allie Frazier," Mother said. "You must be the new tenant who has moved into Mrs. Large's apartment."

"Yes," said the witch. "There's no rocking chair there."

Laura heard Mark and Alex laughing in the back. She was afraid for them. The witch would put a spell on Marm and steal Mark and Alex. She shuddered, thinking of what the witch had said about eating Mark. She stepped up to Marm and whispered, "Should I call the police?"

"No. Oh, no." Marm slid an arm around Laura, binding her there. "This is Laura," Marm said. Laura squirmed but

Marm's grip was firm. "She had one of your popcorn balls the other night."

"I made popcorn balls," the witch said. "Did you come?" She waggled a finger at Laura, and Laura was surprised to see it was not crooked and bony. In fact, there was a baby softness to the hand. "I don't give out twice."

There was a softness to the face, too, Laura noticed. The soft round face with the long scraggly gray hair was creepy, Laura thought. And asking "Did you come?" when Marm had just said Laura had had a popcorn ball. How else would she have gotten one? And then acting as though she knew Laura had come more than once. Laura shivered.

"Which one were you?" the witch asked.

"The Pumpkin Princess," Laura said as quickly as though she had Zipporah's tongue.

"Oh, yes, I remember you," the witch said. "I don't know that story. Will you tell me that story?"

Marm had loosened her grip, and Laura moved away and fled. She ran to Mark and Alex on the back porch, wondering where she could hide them, how she could convince them to hide.

"Look," said Alex, pointing to a butterfly inside the screen.

If only she were a witch, Laura thought, she could turn her brothers into butterflies until the danger was past. She looked down the hall, relieved she could neither see nor hear the witch.

"Let it out, Laura Cat," Mark said, reaching up toward the butterfly, but he wasn't tall enough to catch it. While Laura was wondering if the creature would be better off trapped on the porch or free in the rain, it flitted away from Mark's hand and right into a spiderweb in the corner. Laura reached quickly and cupped it in her hands before it got hopelessly tangled. Now that she had it, she supposed she should let it off the porch. What did butterflies do in the rain?

Making a cage of her fingers, she stepped to the door, pushed it open with her foot, and unclasped her hands. The butterly flew about three feet but was still caught in a spider thread, which was also stuck to Laura's hands. The jewel-winged insect fluttered up and down as though on the end of a tether.

"Look! Look!" she called to her brothers.

"Laura Cat has a pet butterfly," Alex said.

"Let it go, Laura Cat," said Mark.

Laura moved her hand up and down, back and forth, in control of the butterly. Then she reeled it in, freed it of the snare, and watched it fly off through the rain. It was just one small moment of enchantment, but the witch was gone from her mind and from the house.

But the witch returned as part of the conversation at dinner, when Marm told Daddy about the strange visitor. "I phoned Mrs. Large, and apparently the woman—her name is Daurice—had gone through the neighborhood trying doors, walking in, and sitting awhile if there was a rocking chair."

"Let's get rid of it," Laura said, dismissing all the good times she'd had in that chair. The smell of the witch, and perhaps her very flesh, would cling to the fabric forever. Bound there, no doubt, by spider thread. Laura seemed to remember that witches kept spiders for pets. Although her family had never minded spiders at the corners of the porches, Laura wanted to get some bug spray and kill every spider she could find. Spiders caught butterflies. And witches caught children.

"Oh, come now, Laura Cat. She's harmless," Marm said. "Laura Cat ran and locked the door with Daurice inside," she explained to Daddy.

Daddy laughed. "That's rather like locking the barn door after the horse has been stolen, isn't it, Cat?"

"What does that mean?" asked Mark.

"That's not funny," Laura said.

"I didn't say it was funny," Mark said. "I only asked what it means. What does it mean, Daddy?"

"Just what it says, Markoni. You should lock the barn door so the horse won't be stolen."

Laura was suddenly aware of the doors again. She ran from the table and, sure enough, both doors were unlocked. She latched the screen door, then twisted the latch on the deadbolt lock of the front door.

"I can see I'm going to have to learn to use my door key," Daddy said.

The phone rang, and Alex, saying, "Let me, let me," swirled from his bench and scampered to the phone. Smiling, Marm followed, and Mark, Laura, and Daddy listened to the baby voice.

"Hello. Just a minute, please." Without holding the receiver away from his mouth, he spoke to Marm, then to Laura, then to Marm again. "It's for Laura Cat. It's for you, Laura Cat. Did I do it right? Did I?"

The whole family nodded reassurance to Alex, and he nodded reassurance to himself, and Laura went to the phone.

Anna's voice said, "That Alex is so cute."

"Oh, hello, Anna," Laura said.

"We can have it," Anna said.

"Have what?" Laura's mind had been in six thousand places since the afternoon at Anna's.

"The Thanksgiving party," Anna said. "The Thanksgiving party."

Conversations in the Pear Tree

In the school cafeteria the three girls chattered about the Thanksgiving party. There were things to work out, of course, like when to have it.

"Mother suggested the Friday night after Thanksgiving," Anna said.

"But then it won't be on the day," Laura protested.

"Our house will be filled with family all day long." Anna explained. Anna's whole family—grandparents, aunts, uncles, cousins—all lived in Hanover. No Banner had ever moved away. "I couldn't come on Thanksgiving Day even if it was somewhere else."

"And the Sabbath begins on Friday night," Zipporah said. "I go to temple."

Laura and Anna looked at each other in surprise.

"Sabbath. Temple. I'm Jewish, remember?"

Laura remembered. She knew Zipporah went to temple on Friday night; it was just that she never thought about it. It was not a part of her own life. They'd never tried to make plans for Friday night before.

"Saturday night, then," Anna said. "If I can't come Thursday and Zipporah can't come Friday, it'll have to be Saturday. "We can play Pin the Hat on the Pilgrim."

Zipporah groaned. "And charades, too, I'll bet."

"I'm not sure that we can think of that many Thanksgiving titles," Laura said. "But Haim probably has a book called *The Mystery of the Flying Feathered Turkey.*"

"Laura Cat! You come to the house. I'll show you that book."

"And what game will you have, Zip? Carving turkeys?"

"Grrr!" Zipporah said loudly, and a flurry of "Shhhhes" rose up around them. Mr. Norris's experiment had been working very well and no one wanted an infraction of the rules.

That afternoon Anna went on to her own house while Laura stopped by Zipporah's for a minute to see the book.

"I'll wait here," Laura said when Zipporah held the door open for her. Zipporah made a face at Laura and went inside alone. Laura knew that Zipporah didn't like the fact that Laura and Anna were reluctant to come over. It was because of grouchy GiGi, Zipporah's great-grandmother. Laura was uncomfortable even standing here on the porch next to the wheelchair ramp GiGi used. Although Laura had never seen the old woman's legs, she knew that they ended at the shinbone. But GiGi could maneuver that wheelchair faster than most people could move their feet.

"See?" Zipporah said hatefully, returning with the book.

And Laura saw with her own eyes. There really was a book called *The Mystery of the Flying Orange Pumpkin*.

"See?" Zipporah said again, opening the cover to show where Mark had written in block letters: "Happy Birthday to Haim. From Mark Frazier."

"I see," said Laura.

Zipporah slid the small book through the mail slot in the door and accompanied Laura down the street and around the corner to her house. They trailed through Laura's house while Laura set down her school books and checked in with Marm. Then they headed for the pear tree. They weaved their way up through the limbs and settled comfortably onto the branches.

"You can see everywhere," Zipporah said. "It isn't private anymore."

Laura shrugged. Everywhere wasn't very far. Their view was the backs and roofs of the several houses that weren't hidden by old live oaks or ancient azalea hedges.

"The leaves fall off the tree every year, Zipporah," Laura said. It was true that until a month ago they could sit in this tree and be leaf-hidden from the world, but Laura always felt private in the pear tree.

"Well, I know that, Laura Cat!"

"But there are some things that don't change."

"Like what?"

"Like Anna never climbs this tree. Have you noticed?"

Zipporah thought for a moment. "No, I never have. But now that I think of it, she never climbs any trees. She doesn't even climb through Lover's Oak, does she?" Lover's Oak was an enormous broad-limbed, sprawling tree they passed every day on the way to and from school. It was said to have been huge when Oglethorpe founded the colony of Georgia more than two hundred and fifty years ago. Laura and Zipporah, along with most of the schoolchildren from the "Old Town" section of Hanover, had scrambled through it. But not Anna. Never Anna.

"And I know why. Do you?" Laura asked.

"I guess she just doesn't like to climb trees."

"Well, maybe, but the real reason is that you can't climb trees in a skirt."

"Who says?"

"Well, I mean people don't. Anna always wears skirts or dresses. She told me it was a sin to wear pants."

"Oh, she gets that from the Bible, I'll bet," Zipporah said.

Laura was amazed. How did Zipporah know that? "Yes, that's what she said."

"It's in the Torah, too. Something about a woman not wearing men's clothing."

"Marm wears Daddy's shirts," said a voice from below. Mark had climbed up on a keg beneath the tree and was reaching for a limb.

"Go away, Mark," Laura said.

"I don't have to," he said, starting to swing up into the tree. "This is my tree as much as yours."

"Is not," she said, and, fast as any monkey, she scrambled down through the boughs and stomped on the limb next to Mark's small hands. "Especially not now." She tapped her feet rapidly and moved as if the next step would be on top of his hands.

"You can't make me," he said, trying to complete his swing into the tree.

"I can, too," she said, keeping him from finding a place around which to hook his leg. Then, lightly, she pressed her foot onto one of his hands. He howled as though she'd broken sixteen bones, and the outcry brought Marm to the porch.

"Mark, why don't you come around front to the oak tree and let Laura Cat and Zipporah play alone for a while," Marm called.

"See?" Laura hissed at Mark, moving her foot to release his hand. She looked up and grinned and winked at Zipporah.

"Let Laura Cat go to the oak tree," he said without letting go of the limb. But Marm kept talking, persuading, and he finally dropped to the ground.

"You're mean, Laura Cat," he said as he trudged away.

"I wish GiGi would say that," Zipporah said as Laura resumed her perch. "She'd order me to quit pestering Haim and play nicely, like it was my fault." GiGi—whose nickname came from the two G's in "Great-Grandmother"—was there all the time while Zipporah's mother and father worked at their clothing store.

Laura grinned at Zipporah, pleased with Marm's reaction. "Marm likes her own privacy, so she's pretty careful with everyone else's," she said. Actually, the oak tree provided more adventurous climbing now that she was older. Not quite so large and sprawly as Lover's Oak, it nonetheless gave access to the roof of the house. And since some oaks, like live oaks, keep their leaves all year, it cloaked the climber in green all year, too. But the pear tree had been hers since she first rolled the keg under it and climbed it at age four. That very first time, when she had worked her way to the top and poked her head out above pear leaves, a neighbor had come screaming in alarm to Marm. By now Laura knew every inch of the tree, every old limb and every new one.

"You mean you know pants are a sin and you still wear them?" Laura asked, picking up the conversation as though it had not been interrupted.

"I didn't say I thought it was a sin," Zipporah said. "I just said it was in the Torah."

"Is that like the Bible?"

Zipporah hesitated. "Well, yes, sort of," she said. "In fact, the Torah is the first five books of the Bible."

"Does it really say that? Where?" Seeing the words wouldn't make her believe it, but it would show her where Anna got such crazy ideas. Anna's comment still felt so personal, as if she'd peppered Laura with a handful of darts.

"I don't know where," Zipporah said. "But maybe Mom

and Dad know. Or we can call the reference librarian.''

"Who is that?" Laura asked. She saw Mark peering around the corner of the house.

"Yeah, who's that?" he said when he knew he'd been seen.

"Go away, Mark!" she yelled, loud enough for Marm to hear.

"Nobody ever tells me anything," he said, stomping away.

Laura laughed. "We tell him too much, that's what," she said to Zipporah.

"You don't know about the reference librarian?" Zipporah asked. "She's one of the people at the library who will answer all kinds of questions. Now, they won't answer silly stuff or do your schoolwork for you, but you can go down or even call and ask for the reference librarian and she'll answer questions for you."

"Really?" Laura asked. She was a regular at the library and she'd never heard of such a thing. "Are you sure?"

"Sure. They love questions. That's their job."

Questions exploded in Laura's head. There was this problem about the pants. And she had never been satisfied about witches. She'd better not tell Mark about it. He'd go down there with the question jar from the dining-room buffet.

"Here comes the one to ask," Zipporah said.

Laura looked down and saw Anna coming around the corner of the house.

"Come on up, skirt and all," Zipporah said. And to Laura's surprise, Anna did. The full skirt caught on twigs, and Anna didn't climb with ease, but she climbed.

"Where in the Bible does it say that girls aren't supposed to wear pants?" Zipporah asked before Anna was even settled. Anna dashed a look at Laura, then entwined herself among the branches as though she might otherwise fall out. What was that look for? Laura wondered, but she kept her mouth shut. She moved her hands from their resting place and stretched her arms, not holding on to anything, just to show Anna how at ease she was in the tree.

"I don't know exactly where," Anna said, "but it says it's an abomination for a woman to wear a man's clothes."

"But these are *my* clothes," Laura said, tugging at her jeans. She didn't know what an abomination was, but it sounded awful.

"It's a sin for a woman to cut her hair, too," Anna said. She looked away from Zipporah and stared out through the bare tree limbs toward the Martins' picnic shelter. "Or to braid it," she added.

Laura glanced at Zipporah with an amused look, but she was not really amused. Pants or braids aside, there they sat, her two best friends, with their thick, uncut hair. She refrained from reaching up to touch her own thin, short thatch.

"Long hair is a woman's glory. I'm sorry, Laura Cat, but that's what the Bible says." Anna turned her head quickly, and her long hair danced in the air. Laura wished for scissors to cut if off.

In her own defense, Laura stated Zipporah's position. "Zipporah doesn't believe what it says about pants or braids, do you, Zipporah?"

48

Anna looked at Zipporah for a denial of Laura's words.

"Laura Cat," Zipporah said, touching both her coiled braids and her pants, "I guess you and I are terrible sinners."

Anna's hands flew to her mouth. "Zipporah, don't say that!" Laura laughed, but a shiver skittered up her spine.

"Well," Anna said. "Well." She opened her mouth and closed it, squirmed in the tree, then turned the squirm into descent. "I have to go," she said as she climbed down. From the ground she looked up at Zipporah and said, "That's the worst sin of all."

"What is?" Zipporah asked.

"Not to believe what it says in the Bible," Anna whispered, as though even saying such words might also be a sin.

All of History

At the dinner table there were more questions.

"What is 'Torah'?" Mark asked.

"Ma-ark!" Laura said. He had enough questions, she thought, without having to get them from her private conversations.

"The Jewish Bible," Marm said.

"Well, not exactly," Dad said, then shrugged. "But I guess that's close enough for the purpose at hand."

Laura nodded. "So Anna has the Bible and Zipporah has the Torah," she said. "What do we have?"

"We have ourselves," Daddy said.

50

"You know what I mean. Like the Torah or the Bible. What do we have?"

Dad took a bite of meat loaf, and Marm took a bite of salad. They looked at each other over their forks. Alex held his glass of milk with one hand and looked over the rim as though he understood what they were talking about.

"Well?" Laura asked.

Daddy smacked his head with the heel of his hand. Laura sighed. She knew he was going to bore them with all of history again.

"Well," Marm said when she'd finished chewing the bite of salad. "Why don't we continue this discussion later when we're finished with dinner and I've put Alex to bed? And then, Laura, we will continue it further with you when Mark is in bed."

"No," Mark protested. "I want to hear it all."

"You won't understand it," Marm said.

"Yes, I will," he hesitated.

"You'll find it boring," Daddy said.

Mark looked at Marm, and she nodded. He looked at Laura, and she shrugged. "Well, maybe," he said.

After Alex was asleep, they all settled around in the living room, and Dad said, "Well, where were we?"

Mark was sloshed in the beanbag chair he'd dragged from the den. Laura was sitting on the sofa close to Marm. She didn't really like the sofa. The upholstery was thick and woolly and it scratched. But this business about pants and hair affected her and Marm, not Daddy, Mark, or Alex. She wanted

51

to be next to Marm when she heard this part of all history.

"The Bible and the Torah are books that tell about God," Marm said. "Do you know who God is, Mark?"

"Yeah," Mark said. "He's the one lots of people think made everything like sky and trees and us and dogs. But we don't think so."

"Very good, Mark," Daddy said. "Except that it is Marm and I, and many other adults, who don't think so. As you grow up and learn all sorts of things, you and Laura will have to decide for yourselves what you think."

"Alex, too," Mark said.

"Yes. Alex, too," Daddy said.

"It would be fun to be God and make all that stuff," Mark said.

Laura smiled. She'd never thought about it, but, yes, it would be fun. If she'd thought up trees, for instance, she probably would have started out making trees just alike for a while. Then she'd have started making trees with different leaves and different barks and different smells. She thought of the smell of pine and sassafras.

"Who would ever make a pinscher dog?" Mark said.

"Affenpinscher," Laura corrected.

Mark looked at her warily to see whether she was going to repeat her pronunciation lesson. "Laura has hair like an affenpinscher," he said.

"Ohhhh!" She started off the sofa to give him his pinch, but Marm touched her arm in warning.

"We're trying to be serious here," Daddy said.

"Anyway," Marm said. "The Bible tells hundreds of stories about God and how things were for people long ago, and many people believe these stories are true."

"But we don't think so," said Mark.

"Some of the stories are probably true, and others are made-up stories that may teach something that is true," Marm said.

"People who believe these stories are true and who believe God is true have made a religion about God and the Bible."

"What's 'religion'?" Mark asked.

Laura watched Daddy and Marm look at each other, and she was glad she wasn't the parent. She knew they were thinking, How do you explain these things to a seven-year-old? And she was wondering how they were going to explain them to a ten-year-old.

"Church," she said in answer to Mark.

"Oh," Mark said, as though he understood and was satisfied with that answer.

"Chalk one up for Laura," Daddy said, and Laura flushed with pleasure.

"What does that mean?" Mark said. Laura, Marm, and Daddy laughed.

"That means if we had a blackboard and were keeping score of who gives good answers, we would chalk one up for Laura," Daddy said.

"Oh," said Mark again, satisfied.

"You about ready for bed, Mark?" Marm asked, and Laura knew they were getting ready for the ten-year-old stuff.

"Uh-uh," Mark said, shaking his head and not looking a

bit sleepy. He did nestle down in the beanbag, however, as though entrenching himself against possible boredom.

Laura noticed another exchange of glances between her parents—an agreement to let Mark stay. She wasn't surprised. They talked about everything in her family, anyway, though she'd learned long ago that some families did not.

"Well, is there a particular place you want to start, Cat?" Daddy asked. "We're getting into some pretty heavy stuff here."

"Pants," Laura said. "And now hair, too. Not cutting it and not wearing it in braids. Anna says it's in the Bible."

"You don't have to worry about braids, Laura Cat," Mark said. "Your hair isn't long enough."

Daddy stood and crossed to the bookshelf. "I can see we are going to need some particular information here," he said. He took a large book from the shelf, and Laura saw it was a Bible. She was surprised. She didn't know they had one. At Anna's, Anna and her parents each had a Bible of their own, and they kept them in their own rooms, on a table or dresser, not on a bookshelf with other books.

"Here," Daddy said, showing a page to Laura. "It's in a section called First Corinthians. '. . . it be a shame for a woman to be shorn or shaven.' " He read further. " '. . . if a man have long hair, it is a shame unto him. . . . But if a woman have long hair, it is a glory to her.' "

"That's it," Laura said. She could see Anna shaking her head and letting that glory fly all over. She touched her own shorn hair.

54

Marm kissed her hair again. "Your hair is a glory, too. It's the color of peaches and as soft as peach fuzz."

"Affenpinscher peach," Mark said.

Marm nudged Laura to ignore Mark.

"Timothy and Peter in the Bible talk against braiding or plaiting the hair," Daddy said. " 'Broiding,' Timothy calls it."

"I can't see what difference it makes if you cut your hair or don't cut your hair, braid it or don't braid it," Laura said.

"Well, I don't, either," Daddy said, "But sometimes they had sensible reasons for things, even though they may no longer seem sensible to us. The only thing I do know for sure," Daddy continued, "is that no one knows everything."

Laura was not comforted. She was old enough to know that her parents didn't know everything, but she wanted them to. Oh, how she wanted them to. She wanted them to tell her everything, give her every answer. A glimmer came to her. Was this why people made up gods, she wondered, so they could think there was *someone* who knew everything?

"How will I ever know what to believe?" she asked.

"By thinking and learning until you have a feel for what is right for you, Laura Catherine Frazier," Daddy said. "You must try to respect the way other people believe, but don't ever let anyone convince you unless you are convinced yourself. Not even me."

Laura sighed. The whole idea was bewildering and lonely. If she stayed ten years old forever, maybe she wouldn't have to think about it. But because of Anna's pronouncement about sin she was already thinking about it. It was too late to stop thinking about it. She thought, I should have stayed nine.

Daddy was looking through the Bible again, saying, "Clothes, clothes, clothes. No clothes."

"Try raiment," Marm said.

"No raiment."

"What's 'raiment'?" Mark asked.

Even though she didn't know the word, Laura knew it must be a Biblical word for clothes. She said, "Clothes," feeling so very ten years old.

Mark asked for confirmation from their parents. "Is that right?"

"That's right," they both said at once.

"Chalk up another one for Laura Cat," Mark said.

"Adornment? Garment?" Marm suggested.

"Garment. Jackpot," Daddy said. "Deuteronomy 22:5." He flipped the pages backward toward the front of the Bible and read, " 'The woman shall not wear that which pertaineth unto a man, neither shall a man put on a woman's garment.' Allie, I'm going to have to stop wearing your clothes."

Mark and Daddy laughed, and Mark moved into the chair with Daddy. He was almost asleep, Laura noted. She found nothing funny in what Daddy had read or said. Did Anna think jeans were a man's garment? And how did it happen that what Anna believed was affecting her?

"I wonder what they meant?" Daddy said. "I thought men and women both wore robes and sandals in those days."

"I thought so, too, but there had to be some difference for

them to make a statement about it," Marm said, then looked at Laura. "You asleep, baby?"

Laura murmured to indicate she was not asleep, although it was a comfort to be called baby. She wished she were still a baby and didn't have to think about such things as pants and hair and sin. Both mind and body felt heavy, but she was far from asleep. She wondered if the reference librarian would know what men and women wore in Deuteronomy days. Somehow it seemed important to find out

Lost Dog

In the morning Laura dressed in an aqua skirt and a long-sleeved yellow blouse. Then she changed from skirt to jeans.

"You know, Laura Cat," Marm said when she saw Laura had changed, "wearing skirts doesn't mean you are agreeing with Anna's beliefs. If you want to wear a skirt, wear a skirt. There will be more important things to make a protest over."

"I know, Marm," Laura said, standing still while Marm fastened a hairclip to hold down her worst cowlick. "I just changed my mind, that's all." Laura realized they both knew that was a lie. "Pants are warmer," she added. Marm had told them it had turned cool during the night.

With Mark bounding ahead of her, Laura started out for school. At the corner she glanced across at the witch's window. She would like to think the witch burned candles all night and slept all day. Then there would be no danger of finding the woman in the rocking chair again.

Zipporah stood waiting, her book-hugging arms inside the first sweater of the season. Her hair was in "broids." Laura smiled, wondering if Zipporah had combed out her hair, then rebraided it, the same way Laura had changed from skirt to jeans.

"I love the crisp weather," Zipporah said, taking a deep breath of autumn air. "It will pop back warm again in a couple of days, though." The little brothers were having hopping contests. First they raced down the sidewalk to see who could cover a certain distance the fastest; then they counted to see who could hop the longest and the most times.

When they met Anna at the end of the sidewalk to her house, she said nothing about men's garments or braids. "I've decided what game I'm going to have for the Thanksgiving party," she said. " 'I'm going to America and I'll take apples.' "

"What kind of game is that? I thought you were going to do Pin the Hat on the Pilgrim," Laura said.

"It's where each person names something beginning with the next letter of the alphabet," Zipporah said. "Also, you have to name what everyone else said before all the way back to *A*. Such as, 'I'm going to America and I'm taking bananas and apples.' "

"Yeah, that's right, Zipporah," Anna said. "Except I don't think they brought bananas. Bananas don't grow in England."

"England was in trade with India, and bananas grow in India," Zipporah said.

"But even if they were green to start with, they'd be rotten before they got here," Anna said.

"You said, 'I'm going to America,' not 'I've arrived in America.' They had to eat on the way, you know. They didn't exactly have jet travel in those days. Those voyages lasted a long time. Besides, you didn't say it had to be what the Pilgrims brought."

"That's what makes it a Thanksgiving game," Anna said.

"Oh, all right. I'll bring bagels."

"Zipporah!"

With her arms full of books Zipporah couldn't put her hands on her hips, but Laura thought Zipporah's eyes looked as though her hands were on her hips. "Some of the first Jews in America came to Savannah in the colony of Georgia in the 1720s," she said.

"But the Pilgrims came in 1620," Anna said.

"Well, it's close enough," Zipporah said. "They came from England and I'm sure they brought bagels."

Laura's eyes were darting back and forth between them as if she were watching a Ping-Pong match. This was the closest she'd ever seen Anna come to having an argument. And how had Zipporah known the game? she wondered. She'd never heard of it herself, and she knew lots of games. It seemed that no matter what she knew, Zipporah already knew it and more. Including what to believe about sins.

"Go ahead, Laura Cat," Zipporah said. "*C*. Cherries, candy, cauliflower. . . ."

"Oooooh," Anna said. "I hate cauliflower. And they wouldn't have brought that, either. It doesn't keep well at all."

"I know the alphabet," Laura said. "And I know what starts with *C*." She scampered through her thoughts, not wanting to use any of the things Zipporah had suggested, though she was tempted to say *cauliflower* just to annoy Anna. Cantaloupe, cucumbers, she thought, and dismissed them. They wouldn't keep, either. Cradle? No, they'd make one when they needed it. Surely they didn't come all that way with babies— or did they? She imagined the dark interior of a ship and a baby crying.

"Come on, Laura Cat," said Zipporah. "I'm all ready with my next word."

Laura wanted to think of something good enough to shut them up. Two things came to her. "I'm trying to decide," she said, "between candles and calico."

"Ooooh, good, Laura Cat," Anna said.

"But you have to say you're going to America," Zipporah said.

Stubbornness overcame Laura.

"And you have to name the other things, too," Anna said.

"What a stupid game," Laura said. "Just wait until I tell you *my* game. It's the best ever." She looked ahead of them. The boys had just climbed through Lover's Oak and were

hopping again. Mark hopped twelve times before he tottered.
"Your game is probably stupid, too," Zipporah said.
"Oh, I'll bet it's not," Anna said. "Laura Cat is good at games."

Anna's kind response irritated Laura more than Zipporah's snippy one. "I can hop forever if I want to," she said. She took off, hopping down the sidewalk, down and up the curb, until she was way ahead.

After school, Laura clasped her books to her chest and walked along in silence while Anna and Zipporah chattered away. For once, Mark had met her in the schoolyard and started walking along just ahead.

"Go on home, you brat," she said.

"You're the brat," he answered, and he started dawdling behind. A man was half blocking the sidewalk, and so they had to pass in single file.

"Here, Blackie! Here, Blackie!" the man called. "I've lost my dog," he said to them. "Will you girls help me find my dog?"

Find your own dog, Laura thought, while both Anna and Zipporah "Oooohed" and said, "I hope you find it," and quickly glanced toward neighboring yards.

"I sure would hate it if we lost Schnitzy," Zipporah said.

"Haim would die, I bet," Anna said.

Schnitzy, short for Wienerschnitzel. Laura thought it was a stupid, idiotic name for a stupid, idiotic-looking dog. And her hair did not look like an affenpinscher's, either. She put a hand to it to smooth it down.

"You were mean to Marky," Zipporah said.

"Well, when did you turn into an angel?" Laura asked, biting her tongue to keep from adding, "Zip." *Marky. The twins.* It seemed Zipporah called everyone whatever she chose whether anyone liked it or not, but no one better call her "Zip." She'd heard Zip be mean to Haim plenty of times.

Zipporah stopped by Anna's to see "the twins," and Laura walked on alone. Today she though those two little girls were awful. If one of them knocked over her block tower, she'd knock her block off. And then she really would be a sinner.

At home she flopped facedown on her bed, with her arms folded under her head. She took a deep breath, determined never to let it out. Eventually it burst out of its own accord, and it sounded like a soul-killing sigh. She took another breath, dragging in as much air as she could. Then, when she could no longer hold it, she snorted it out. If she could hold her breath for long enough, she thought the air might cause a draft inside her head and blow out all her troubled thoughts. When she almost had herself blank and floating, Marm interrupted.

"Laura Cat, have you seen Mark?"

"He was just behind me," she said quietly, using as little breath as possible, trying to say the words and still keep aloft.

"Well, he probably stopped off at Haim's. I'll call and have him come home. I don't want him over there pestering GiGi with his questions. She's too old."

Called up by Marm's words, GiGi drifted into Laura's head,

wheelchair and all, floating, turning over and over without falling out of the chair. Laura shivered and shook herself out of the reverie. How had she let GiGi get into her mind? GiGi was the oldest, crabbiest person Laura had ever known. The old woman's skin was so crackled she looked like a human jigsaw puzzle. Now *there* was a witch, Laura thought. There was someone who would eat Mark for dinner. There was the reason they usually played at Laura's, sometimes at Anna's, but hardly ever at Zipporah's.

"Tell me where you last saw Mark," Marm said, standing in the doorway again. "He's not at the Greengolds'. GiGi was about to call me. Haim is not home, either."

"They're probably playing with Betsy and Bonnie," Laura said. "That's where Zipporah is."

"No, I've already checked with Mrs. Banner. Zipporah is there, but not Mark or Haim."

A picture came to Laura's mind of the boys hopping down the sidewalk ahead of her. And while they were hop-hop-hopping in her mind's eye, she also saw the morning sun. As they walked toward Queen Street and school, the sun had been to the right. It was this morning when they were hopping. She was stricken with the knowledge that she had not paid any attention to them this afternoon. Her own bad mood had eclipsed everything else

"Will you stay with Alex while I walk around and look a bit?" Marm asked. "I'm not really worried about him or anything, I just want him home."

Laura shuffled into the den, where Alex was playing with

blocks. She remembered a day she hadn't come straight home. She'd been seven and in second grade, just like Mark.

"Make me a bridge," Alex said as soon as he saw her. He was long past the stacking and knocking-down stage. In fact, he'd built a fairly elaborate system of roads and ramps for his cars. Instead of making a bridge for him, she told him which blocks to use and how to make it himself.

The day she hadn't come home was a day when a classmate who lived near school had invited her over to play. She hadn't meant to stay so long. She was only going to see where the girl lived so she could go home and tell Marm and ask permission. But there was a real playhouse in the backyard, with furniture and a rug, and curtains at the window. Without even deciding to, they began to play house. After a while the girl's mother came to check and asked Laura if her mother knew where she was. With a start, Laura jumped up and ran for home. She met Marm on the sidewalk, walking along with Alex in the stroller and Mark holding her hand. "I don't know whether to kiss you or kill you," Marm had said.

Marm came down the hall now. "Have they shown up yet?"

Laura shook her head, wondering whether Mark was going to be kissed or killed.

"Well, I've called the Greengolds at the store, but the little rapscallions have not been there."

"I'll bet they are in town, though," Laura said. It struck her as exactly the place two adventurous seven-year-olds would go on a day they'd decided not to come straight home from school.

Marm tilted her head. "Maybe so. I hope so."

A twinge of guilt pinched Laura. She should have been keeping her eye out. Now Marm would be mad and Mark would be in trouble, and she could have prevented it.

"I'm not really worried. I don't have a feeling that anything has happened to them," Marm said. "But if they don't show up in five minutes, I am calling the p-o-l-i-c-e."

Alex, instantly aware of the sound of spelling, said, "I know what that is. Coca-Cola. Can I have some?"

Marm winked at Laura. "Yes. Laura Cat will get it for you," she said, and walked away.

As Laura poured Coke over ice, the telephone rang. She expected to hear Marm's running feet, and when she didn't, she handed the glass to Alex and ran to answer it herself.

"Hello," she said, grabbing the receiver before the fourth ring.

"Mrs. Frazier, please," a man's voice said.

"She can't come to the phone right now," Laura said. She pulled the long coil of cord toward the living room and looked out across porch and yard. She had been taught never to say her parents were not at home.

"Mr. Frazier, then?" the voice asked.

"He's not here right now," she said, feeling safe enough to have Marm at home.

"Uh, well, tell her it's important," the man said. "It's about her son Mark."

Laura clanked the telephone down and fled to the front door, screaming, "Marm! Marm!" Mark was hurt or dead, lying crumpled in the street, hit by a car. Or drowned in the river, soaked through to the bone marrow. Why hadn't they thought of the river? Of course the boys would head for the river. And it was her fault.

She banged open the front door, her mouth wide with shouting. Then Marm was running across the yard.

"Telephone!" Laura yelled, feeling her heart beating in her ribcage and a lump in her throat. "It's about Mark!"

Marm seemed to reach the porch in one leap and the phone in two. During the phone conversation Marm kept flapping her hand as though to shush Laura, though Laura wasn't making a sound. "Yes . . . Yes . . . Yes . . . Oh, my!" Marm said. "Where? . . . Where is that? . . . Yes . . . Okay . . . Okay . . . Twenty minutes. It will take me about twenty minutes."

As soon as Marm put down the phone, Laura clamored, "What is it? Where are they? Are they all right?"

"Laura Cat, shut up," Marm said.

Laura shut.

"Let me see, let me think," Marm said. "I have to call the Greengolds. I have to call your father. Laura Cat, they've been *kidnapped.*"

All's Well That
Ends Well

The lump in Laura's throat slid down to her stomach, down her left thigh to her toes, then sprang upward again. She almost threw up right there in the hall. It was both better and worse than she'd thought. At least the boys were alive. For now.

"Oh, Laura Cat, I'm sorry. They're all right." Marm hugged her quickly. "They're all right. I should have told you that. It's over. They're safe. They are safe now." Marm's finger whirled in the dial. She asked for Daddy. He wasn't there. She left a message for him to meet her at the police station because there was an emergency. She called the Greengolds. "We've found the boys. They're out near Interstate 95. I'll be by to get you in three minutes.'' She clunked down the phone. ''Laura Cat, you stay with Alex.''

''No-o-o,'' Laura wailed. Mark might be safe, but she didn't feel safe. It was as though she and Alex would be kidnapped if Marm left them. Whatever happened to Mark had been her fault because she hadn't been watching. She didn't want to be responsible for watching Alex.

''Alex, come,'' Marm said instantly. She grabbed him up and ran to the car, with Laura right behind. The car jerked out of the driveway, Marm talking to herself every minute. ''Allie, calm down. Take it easy, Allie, don't have a wreck.'' The car bounced down the street, and Laura, looking at Marm's foot, saw it was bouncing on the gas pedal.

''Calm down, Marm,'' Laura said, and didn't know where the words came from. She was shaking all over, as though every muscle and bone had turned to water and she were going to slosh right out of herself. ''Are they really all right?'' she asked. Maybe Marm wasn't telling her the truth. Maybe the person who phoned hadn't been telling the truth.

''Yes, Laura Cat, they're safe. They're all right. Shut up, darling. Please be quiet.''

The Greengolds were standing at the curb. The store was closed and locked behind them. They climbed into the backseat and Marm sped off, heading south toward the river bridge. Laura listened as Marm told the Greengolds what she knew.

''This man—omigod I've forgotten his name! He has them at the Mini-Mart near I-95. Do you know it?'' They didn't.

''They build a new one every day,'' said Mr. Greengold.

69

"He said it was the old one. He said we couldn't miss it." At least Marm's foot had stopped shaking and she was driving smoothly. "He said when he drove by them they were just walking along with their schoolbooks. It was a woodsy area, no place for two small children to be walking alone." She stopped talking a moment to catch her breath. "It bothered him, he said, and after a couple of miles he turned back and there they were, these two tiny boys, still trudging along. He stopped and spoke to them, and they said they'd come from school with a man and he'd put them out here. He said that's what scared him the most, that they had apparently been picked up by a stranger at school and were so ready and willing to talk to another stranger."

Laura's slosh turned to ice. She stared out the window as they crossed the bridge, not seeing river or marsh or distant islands. What if the man who had called was the kidnapper and not the rescuer at all? What if he were trying to get them all out there to kidnap them all? She should have stayed home with Alex. Then at least two of them would be safe.

"Are the police meeting us there?" asked Mr. Greengold. Marm zoomed down from the bridge, passed the road to Golden Isle on the left and the duck pond on the right.

"Omigod," Marm said.

"What? What?" asked everyone else, even Alex.

"I didn't call the police. Poor Dan. I left a message for Dan to meet us at the police station and I didn't call the police. He'll be terrified out of his mind. He won't know what has happened. He won't know everyone is safe."

"It's all right," said Mr. Greengold. "We can stop and call."

Marm zipped past the marsh until they were on the mainland again, with woods on both sides of the highway and no houses anywhere. "I don't think there is anywhere to call from," she said. "He said it was the first store, just before the intersection of I-95 to Jacksonville."

Jacksonville sounded like a foreign country to Laura instead of the nearest city, in Florida, the next, nearby state.

"How do you know this man was telling the truth?" Mr. Greengold asked, expressing Laura's fear. "What if he's the kidnapper?"

All the adults stopped breathing for ten full seconds.

"You'd better call the police," Mrs. Greengold said. "What do you think?"

"Yes, Allie, turn around and let's find a phone," Mr. Greengold said.

Marm shook her head. "I'm not turning around," she said. "If we pass a place to call, we will call, but I'm not turning around. I mean to get closer and closer to my child, not go back the other way."

"Yes," said Mrs. Greengold. "Me, too."

"What if?" Mr. Greengold said, and they drove for a minute in the fear of the "what if."

"I'll run over him," Marm said. "I'll smash through the store. I will yank him bald and claw his eyes out."

When they saw a store ahead, everyone again held their breath. Already in view, standing by the gas pumps, was a

71

man with two little boys. Marm took a deep breath and reached out and touched Laura's hand. "Be calm, now," she said. "Everyone, be calm."

The man's name must have come to her because as she stepped out of the car Marm spoke it, with a question mark.

"Yes," he said.

"What took you so long?" Mark asked. "Haim was scared."

"I wasn't scared," said Haim. "*You* were scared."

"What took *us* so long, buddy boy?" Marm asked. "What took *you* so long? It's four-fifteen and you haven't been home from school yet."

"We were helping a man look for his dog," Haim said. Everybody held their breath, except for Laura, who expelled hers. "Here, Blackie! Here, Blackie!" rang in her ears.

"He said he'd give us a white rabbit if we helped him find his dog."

The man was thanked and thanked and thanked again while the boys were piled into the car, Haim in back with his parents and Mark up front with Laura, Alex, and Marm. Mark jabbered all the way to town, with small additions from Haim in the backseat. They had looked for the dog around school, and then the man had suggested they ride around to look from the car.

"Didn't it occur to you not to get in a car with a stranger?" Mrs. Greengold asked.

"Not now, dear," said Mr. Greengold. "Don't put them on the defensive. We need to get every scrap of information we can."

"He was a painter," Mark said. "A housepainter."

"Did he tell you that?" Marm asked.

"No, but he was dressed in white coveralls and had paint all over his shoes."

Daddy and a policeman were standing in front of the police station. Daddy grabbed them all in one big hug almost before they were out of the car.

"You're safe, you're all safe!" he said, almost crying.

"Oh, Dan. I'm sorry to have terrified you like this. I'm so sorry I didn't leave a better message. The boys were kidnapped. Mark and Haim were kidnapped from near school."

Mark and Haim told their story again, repeating what they'd already said and telling more.

"Anna, Zipporah, and I saw the man looking for his dog," Laura said. "He asked us to help." She shivered. What if they had helped? They would have known better than to get in the car, and Mark and Haim could have gotten past him. "I thought Mark was already ahead of us," she said. All sorts of sharp-pointed feelings poked her from inside. Now she did feel sinful. She felt all full of evil.

The police were amazed at the details Mark gave about the man and his car, describing both in detail.

"His car radio wouldn't work," Mark said.

"How do you know that?" a policeman asked.

"Because I turned it on to WHAN and it didn't work. It wasn't the antenna. He had a tall antenna and it wasn't broken."

"Mark wouldn't shut up asking questions," Haim said. "The man got mad and made us get out."

Marm and Daddy nearly squeezed Mark in half. "You keep right on asking those questions," Daddy said.

"Yeah, Mark," Laura said. "Fill up that jar with questions. We'll answer every one."

"That's the only time I was scared," Mark said. "When he made us get out and we didn't know where we were and there were no houses anywhere. I almost started to cry. But Haim said to walk, so we walked."

The adults kept saying, "All's well that ends well," till Laura thought she would scream. Mark and Haim were safe, but nothing else was well.

"We'll put out an all-points bulletin," the police said. "We'll keep you informed. You call us if the boys come up with anything else that might be helpful."

They dropped the Greengolds off at the store and drove home. The five of them walked up the front walk with their arms all wrapped around one another.

"We're all here together," Daddy said. "Mark, Alex, Laura Cat, and My Nose." He kissed Marm on the nose, then suddenly laughed.

"I'm glad you can find the relief of laughter in this," Marm said.

"I left my car at the police station," he said.

They all laughed, and it *was* a relief. They fell all over each other and all over the walk. Daddy's leaving the car at the police station became the funniest thing that had ever happened.

"I'll take you back," Marm said.

"No," Daddy said. "Leave it." And the thought of leaving it was even funnier.

With Alex in his arms, Daddy stepped ahead of the rest of them and opened the door. Laura was the first one in—and there was the witch, sitting in the rocking chair, rocking, rocking, rocking.

Mark's Watchdog

The moment Laura saw her, she knew. The witch was the one who had taken the boys from school. She had turned herself from a short, pale, pasty woman into a lean, dark-haired man who had stood there on the sidewalk calling, "Blackie! Blackie!"

"Well, hello, Daurice," Marm said, pushing Laura into the room as she came in with Mark.

Laura looked from Daddy to Marm, wondering why they didn't see what she saw. This was the woman who had said she ate boys like Mark for Thanksgiving. The witch probably had a room full of white rabbits there in Mrs. Large's apartment with all the candles. Their lack of recognition put fear into her again, as though they were responsible, too, like the father who poisoned his children's Halloween candy. The more unreasonable it was, the more reasonable it seemed.

"Did you find the boy?" Daurice asked, without breaking the rhythm of her rocking.

"Here he is," Daddy said, playfully pulling Mark to his side. What was wrong with the woman, Laura wondered, asking such a question with Mark right there?

"All's well that ends well," Alex announced, and he crossed the room and climbed into the witch's lap. Marm, Daddy, and Mark collapsed on this or that piece of furniture. Only Laura stood, feeling older than any of them, old enough to see how very young Alex was to be so casual about laps.

"I was worried," said Daurice, rocking, rocking.

"We appreciate your concern," Marm said.

She is the cause of our concern, Laura thought. How did the witch know about Mark? It was over before anyone knew what was happening. I want her out of my house, she wanted to shout. I want her out of my house. Even though she knew she was being rude, the words spurted out of her like a breath held too long.

"I want her out of our house!"

"Laura!" said both parents at once.

"I do," Laura said. "I want her out of my house."

They didn't exclaim her name again. Acting as if he hadn't heard her cry out, Daddy stood up and stretched as casually as anything. "What say we go out for a bite to eat? I don't think either of us wants to get in that kitchen tonight."

"Yay-yay-yay!" Alex and Mark shouted, covering Daddy's words even before he finished. Alex slid down from the witch's lap. On top of the whoops came a string of suggestions about where to go. Laura held her breath. If they could go right this minute, get this woman out of the house right now, maybe she would be all right.

"Would you like to join us, Daurice?" Daddy asked. The words sliced through Laura's stomach.

"Sir?" Daurice said.

He repeated the invitation. Alex shouted, "Yay!" again and ran back to the witch and tugged at her hand. Laura didn't move, didn't breathe. It seemed she'd been holding her breath this whole livelong day. If she let it out, she would fly into three hundred and sixteen pieces. If they ever got her put back together again, she would be like GiGi.

"Well, let's go. Time's awasting," Daddy said, moving toward the door. Alex pulled on Daurice until she stood up, and they walked to the door. Mark and Marm stood and went to the door.

"Laura?" Daddy said when he'd ushered the others onto the porch.

She noted that he'd left off the "Cat," as he had when he and Marm both called her name a minute ago. She shook her head. She was not capable of making a sound.

"Come on, Sugarpuss," he said.

Laura shook her head again. She saw Daddy glance to the porch. Marm was standing in the doorway. The boys and the witch were walking to the car.

78

"Not with her," Laura managed to say, letting out her breath and not flying apart after all.

"She's going to be our guest," Marm said. "She needs some friends."

Laura's words were gone. She was back to shaking her head.

"I'm sorry you're upset," Daddy said. "It's been a hard but joyful day. And maybe this wasn't the best time for us to invite Daurice, but this was when the occasion arose, and I won't take back the invitation now. Come on, Cat." He bobbed his head in a come-along motion. "Come on, Sugar-apple-dumpling-puss."

She could not, would not. Her fears skewered her to the floor.

"Okay, baby. I'm not going to make you. You've been saying you're old enough to stay by yourself, so we'll let you. We'll be back in an hour, and we'll bring you something, okay?"

He stepped through the doorway and across the porch. With her whole heart she wanted to follow, but her feet wouldn't move. She wanted to call, "Wait!" but her lips and throat wouldn't move, either. Huge walloping tears plopped onto her cheeks.

Gray dark was pressing against the windows. She had been cast off. They had left her behind in favor of the witch.

They brought her a hamburger, French fries, and Coke that kidnapping night. The witch was not with them when they returned. Still, the smell of candle wax and rabbits was in the food, and Laura could not eat it. She made a peanut-butter-and-jelly sandwich instead.

She became Mark's watchdog. And almost every day, when she came home from school, there was the witch sitting in the rocking chair, rocking, rocking.

She was surprised she didn't have nightmares about it, but the daymares were intense. Laura was sure that the witch was somehow responsible for what had happened, but no one believed her. What's more, she knew that she was responsible, too. Marm and Daddy told her and told her that it was not her fault. "No one can watch a person every minute, and no one should be expected to," they said. They told her she was being ridiculous to blame herself and unfair to blame Daurice. It was not her fault, they repeated. But no matter what they said, she knew they blamed her. She should have been watching.

On the way to and from school she stayed behind Mark as he and Haim hopped, skipped, jumped, twirled, or ran down the sidewalk. If Zipporah and Anna were slow, she walked on without them, and she even followed Mark to his classroom to be sure he was safely inside. Danger could be anywhere. Even in the school hall there could be witches bewitching boys to look for lost things.

Laura began bypassing her own front door and coming into the house through the kitchen. Once inside, she'd find Marm and hiss the question "Is she here?"

The first few times Marm answered "Yes"or "No." Depending on the answer, Laura would retreat uneasily to her room or relax and roam the house freely. Then Marm began saying, "Laura, you're being absurd about this. See for yourself." If Laura asked Mark or Alex, they only gave a repetition of Marm's reply.

Alex even turned it into a singsong chant: "See for yourse-elf, see for yourse-elf, Laura Cat's an e-elf."

Unless she knew whether or not the witch was rocking, she could not even settle in her own room. She began creeping down the hall and peeping into the living room. She dreaded catching the witch's eye. But the witch, when she was there, was always staring straight ahead to where a watercolor of sea gulls hung. The woman seemed to be looking not at the picture but into space, seeing things that only witches can see. The witch's feet pushed against the apple-green carpet and kept the chair rocking, rocking. Only on days when the chair was empty did the heaviness leave Laura's chest.

After the initial excitement, even Zipporah seemed unconcerned. "All's well that ends well," she said.

"If one more person says that, I'll spit," Laura said.

"All's well that ends well," said Zipporah.

Laura spat.

"Anna is going to give parties for a career. What are you going to do? Be Mark's bodyguard? Go to high school with him? You can go into business, Laura Cat. Put up a sign. 'Professional Worrier.' You can charge people money for bringing their worries to you so they don't have to worry themselves. You'll be rich, Laura Cat."

"I know I'd worry about Betsy and Bonnie," Anna said,

looking at Laura with sympathy. "If anything like that ever happened to them, I'd watch them every minute."

"The time to watch is before it happens." Laura snapped, recalling Daddy's comment about locking the barn door. "You didn't even know about it until it was over, Zipporah. You didn't have time to be scared. If you had, then you would be more understanding."

"Yeah," Anna said. "I think so, too."

Even Mark—especially Mark—was unappreciative of her caring.

"Make Laura Cat stop watching me," he complained to Marm. "She acts like my personal spy."

"Don't hover, Laura Cat," Marm said for the umpteenth time.

"But the stupid little jerk will go with the next person who acts like they've lost a dog," Laura said. Neither of the boys had shown the least fear of the man who had picked them up. They weren't afraid until he put them out, until they were really safe.

Marm signaled above Mark's head, and Laura shut up. She had heard all their reasons. They were trying to make him careful without turning him into a fearful person. Laura thought it would do him good to be a little fearful.

She kept herself upside-down as much as possible, hanging by her knees from the pear tree until her face was the color of a plum. She worked out an intricate cartwheel path around and around the tree, wondering whether she could learn to cartwheel fast enough to turn herself into butter. In her room she stood on her head until her blood was pulsing behind her eyeballs.

"Laura Cat, you're going to make yourself sick," Marm warned.

How could she explain that the only time everything seemed right-side-up was when she was upside-down?

And every night, candles. Zipporah said the witch still burned them every night. Laura began going for walks after supper to see for herself. There was a brief discussion about whether she should be allowed to walk alone after dark. Marm said, "If it keeps her on her feet so the blood can settle, let her."

Four nights in a row she walked to the corner and sat on the curb. Across the street in the second house, candles glowed from every upstairs window. Once she saw the witch herself, making strange shadowy movements above the candles. Was she doing black magic or was she sending signals? And who was she sending them to?

Laura
Upside-Down

The day before Thanksgiving, Laura learned that the witch had been invited for Thanksgiving dinner.

"I won't be here," she snapped. She crossed her arms and locked them tightly. "I'm going to Grandma's," she said through clenched teeth, regretting the stupidity of her statement as soon as she'd made it. Grandma didn't live here in Hanover like all of Anna's relatives. Grandma lived six hundred miles away in Maryland. Besides, how could she help Mark if she wasn't here?

"You will be right here at our table, and you will be polite to our guest," Marm said firmly.

With unaccustomed roughness, Daddy clamped his hand

around her upper arm as though he were going for the bone. "You will sit at our Thanksgiving table in pleasant celebration," he said.

"I'll be sick," she answered, still not parting her teeth. How could he tell her to be pleasant so unpleasantly? she wondered.

"We will prop you up and keep you at the table," he went on. "Even if you are sick and dying. We'll take you to the emergency ward or the funeral parlor after dinner." He released his grip.

"I'm already sick," she said, and then she ran out to the pear tree and tangled herself in its limbs. She stared blankly east, then west. From the upstairs rooms at Anna's house, one could see the marsh to the east and the river to the west. From here the view was concealed by tall houses and trees. There had been a few chilly days but no cold ones yet, and today the sun was trying to say "Summer." "That's what I like about the South," Daddy always said on these bare-arm Georgia days.

Laura didn't feel summery, but after a long while she did get an idea of what she could do about tomorrow. She would pretend. She would pretend she wasn't there. Or pretend the witch wasn't there. Then she pictured them at the table and knew it would be impossible. Marm and Daddy would be at either end, and she would be next to or across from the witch.

She turned things over in her mind to see if there was any way to avoid being at the table tomorrow. She could die in bed, and they would spend the day grieving and blaming themselves. The idea was momentarily delicious, but then she thought Daddy would sit her corpse at the table and that would spoil her reason for dying. Also, if she was dead she would miss the Thanksgiving party on Saturday. She'd bragged about her game and she had not even thought of one yet. Maybe dying was a good idea after all. Or maybe she would think about games while she was at the table.

Suddenly, she had a new idea. If she couldn't go to Grandma's, she could pretend Grandma was here. In her mind she could turn the witch into Grandma. There was a rush of apologetic feeling toward Grandma, but Grandma would understand. And it just might work. To test it she spoke quietly, but aloud, to herself. "Grandma's coming. Grandma's coming." It was amazing. Already she felt better.

Then her spirits sank again. Grandma always made a dessert called cranberry mousse. It was a cross between a custard and ice cream, and it was Grandma's specialty. How could she pretend Grandma was here if there was no cranberry mousse? She wondered if Marm would make it. Then she could pretend Grandma had made it. She let the idea wander around her head a bit until it settled; then she climbed down from the tree and strolled inside the house.

"Could we have cranberry mousse for dessert tomorrow?" she asked.

"Well, your daddy already has two pumpkin pies in the freezer," Marm said.

"Couldn't we have both?"

"I don't know how to make it," Marm said. "That's your Grandma's specialty."

"Couldn't you call her?"

"Laura Cat, that's a fine idea." Marm kissed the tip of a finger and touched it to Laura's nose. "But how about this? Why don't *you* call for the recipe? If it's not too difficult, you can make it yourself, and it can become your specialty, too."

The idea floated to Laura like a cumulus cloud and surrounded her with a feeling of white lightness. The relief was as wonderful as their laughter on the sidewalk when Daddy left his car at the police station.

Grandma was delighted to hear Laura's voice and even more pleased to share the recipe. Laura wrote the ingredients and instructions carefully, then called Marm to double-check everything before she hung up. Marm took her downtown to Mitchell's Market and helped her find the right aisles but let Laura take everything off the shelves herself.

When Mark saw Laura in the kitchen surrounded by ingredients, he said, "That's not fair. What do I get to make?"

"What would you like to make?" Marm asked.

"Mashed potatoes," Mark said.

"All right, you can do that with Daddy," Marm said. "But they'll have to be done fresh tomorrow, just before dinner."

"Yay, yay, ya-a-ay!" Mark said, twirling and trailing his voice behind him.

Under Marm's supervision Laura combined the right quantities of cranberry sauce, condensed milk, sugar, and lemon juice, and poured the mixture into cake tins. It was supposed to freeze, then be beaten again.

"Don't tell anyone I made it," Laura said.

"Well, Laura Cat, everyone already knows you're making it."

"Yeah, Laura Cat, I know," said Alex, who had dragged his blocks and cars into the kitchen.

Laura struggled to express what she meant. "I mean, don't tell *her.*"

"Her who?" Marm said.

Laura squirmed. She knew that Marm knew who. "Who" was the only other person coming for Thanksgiving dinner. And "who" had to be Grandma in Laura's mind. But if "who" knew that Laura had made the mousse, then Grandma could not have made it.

"You know," Laura said.

"She has a name, Laura Cat," Marm said. "I refuse to hear what you are saying unless you use her name. She is going to be our guest."

Laura opened the freezer door and touched a finger to the mousse, as though it might already be frozen in two minutes. She licked the dot of mousse from her finger, then took a deep breath, hoping it would not be bad luck to say the witch's name.

"Will you please not tell Daurice I made the mousse?" The name penetrated her tongue with the bitterness of that mealy marrow that separates the two halves of a pecan.

"You've done a lovely job with it," Marm said. "I don't

know why you don't want her to know you made it, but I will not tell her."

"And will you please tell other people not to tell?" She looked pointedly at Alex, who was looking back with a spark in his eyes. She could just hear him announcing, "Laura Cat said not to tell you she made the mousse."

Marm talked to Alex about it until there could be no mistake that he understood what it was he was not to say.

Dinner was not until one o'clock, so Laura had all Thanksgiving morning to dread the arrival of the witch. While Daddy and Mark peeled, cooked, and mashed the potatoes, Laura was in a corner of her room, standing on her head. When a knock came at the front door, she bent her knees to her chest, then to the floor, stood up, and slipped into the hall. Knowing exactly what was said might help her protect them against spells.

Beyond Marm's back she could see one side of the witch's head, hair as gray and thin as ever, but combed.

"For us? Thank you. How thoughtful. Isn't it beautiful?" Marm was saying.

Laura couldn't see what it was the witch had brought. Whatever it was, they would have to beware. Marm backed away from the door, and the witch immediately crossed to the rocker. As Marm turned, Laura saw she was holding an elaborate candle that looked like a cascade of brown, yellow, and orange ribbons. Where had the witch got such a magnificent candle?

Marm saw Laura at the edge of the hall and held the candle toward her. "See the candle Daurice brought? Do come and say hello, Laura Cat."

The look in Marm's eyes was as full of steel as Daddy's grip on her arm had been. Laura knew she had to move forward at once. You're pretending, remember? she said to herself. That's Grandma who brought the candle. She got her legs moving, stepped forward into the living room, and "Hello" came out of her mouth quite respectably. She even managed to add, "That's a nice candle."

"I make them," the witch said.

"You made this yourself?" Marm asked.

Something wavered in Laura. Witches weren't supposed to create beautiful things, only ugly ones. But beautiful things would be more enticing, she reasoned. Inside the candle, she was certain, was a spell for girls who faked politeness.

"It's beautiful," Laura said, the words slipping out as though coaxed by some magic charm. It's Grandma, she reminded herself quickly. She'd only said it to Grandma. Grandma makes candles and cranberry mousse.

"Where I, uh, was before," the witch said, "I learned to make candles."

Laura shivered, not daring to ask where the witch had been "before." Where did witches come from? Was there a certain place where they all gathered to learn how to mix potions and make candles?

Mark came in and announced, "The potatoes are ready."

"Good, too. I had some," said Alex, who'd followed Mark.

He saw the witch and scampered to her and climbed onto her lap.

"Dinner is ready," said Daddy, who had followed Alex.

"Look at the candle Daurice brought," Marm said. "She made it."

"Marvelous," Daddy said.

"For us?" Alex asked, looking into the witch's face.

"I have hundreds," the witch said.

Laura thought someone should snatch Alex from the witch's lap before she sucked out his spirit. The sooner everyone went to dinner, the better. "Daddy said dinner is ready," she announced. "I'm going to wash my hands."

So that's why the witch was always burning candles, Laura thought as she soaped her hands. She has hundreds. While she rinsed, she thought, It's Grandma, It's Grandma, it's Grandma.

At his own request, Alex was seated on his high bench next to the witch. This put Laura across the table, next to Mark. She felt a twinge of guilt for her relief at not having to sit next to the witch, because that put Alex at risk. It was just as awful, she decided, having to sit across from her and find some way to avoid looking her in the eye.

"Daurice, we go around the table, each naming something we're thankful for," Marm said. She didn't say they went round and round and didn't allow repeats. "Laura Cat, will you begin?"

"I'm thankful for Mark," she said, staring boldly at Daurice, sending the message that any spell Daurice could cast, she, Laura Catherine Frazier, could break. Mark looked at Laura in surprise. He still did not comprehend what had so nearly happened to him. The police said if the man had taken only one child, or if Mark hadn't been so talkative and inquisitive, the boys might never have been found at all, much less set free. The police had no leads on the man except that he seemed to be moving up the coast. The week before Mark and Haim's abduction, there had been a report from Miami that a man was trying to get children to go with him by promising them a white rabbit. And from New Jersey, the week after, came a similar report.

"I'm thankful for Mark, too," Daddy said. No one said, "No repeats."

"I'm thankful for Mark, too," Alex said, nodding his head. "I really am, Mark."

Daurice said, "I'm thankful to be here."

"I'm thankful Daurice is here," Marm said. "And I'm thankful for Mark."

"That's two thankfuls, Marm," Mark said. Then he ducked his head and grinned and said, "I'm thankful for me, too."

"Laura Cat?" Daddy prompted, when she didn't go on with her second turn. With the witch sitting across from her, all she could think of was counteracting the witch's power.

"I'm thankful Mark is safe," she said, still staring across the table. And this family will keep him safe, her stare was saying to the witch.

Daddy was thankful that everyone at the table was together. Alex was thankful for the blue, blue sky, and Daurice

92

was thankful for being here. Marm was thankful for having work she loved, and Mark was thankful they finally had a color television set. "After everyone else in the whole wide world," he added.

Laura was stuck. The witch's power had paralyzed her; she couldn't think of anything except that Mark was safe, and she'd said that twice already. Quickly, she leaned over and kissed the side of Mark's head. "I love you, Mark," she said.

"Oh, yuck, Laura Cat, yuck, yuck," he said, rubbing his head to be rid of her kiss.

"I'm thankful that people are free to say yuck without being sent from the table," Daddy said. They all knew it was a real thankful and not a scolding. Daddy had told them of many instances of being sent from the table for no good reason when he was a boy.

"I'm thankful for the green, green trees," Alex said.

Daurice was thankful for being here, Mother was thankful for all the love she felt around the table, and, mocking Alex, Mark said, "I'm thankful for the brown, brown turkey, and I hope we can eat it now."

Daddy started carving.

During dessert the witch asked, "Who made this?"

Laura almost swallowed her tongue along with a mouthful of mousse. Her eyes darted to each family member, but even while she was giving a don't-you-dare look at Alex, Mark and Marm were both speaking.

"I made the mashed potatoes," Mark said.

"It's called cranberry mousse," Marm said. "It's an old recipe of my mother's."

Marm's answer seemed to satisfy the witch. "It's good," she said.

After dinner they traipsed back and forth between the dining room and the kitchen, clearing the table, washing the dishes. Alex climbed onto the kitchen stool and helped wash the silverware. The witch helped, too, carrying the turkey platter, then the glasses, just as if she were Grandma and really a part of the family. Laura was startled to realize she was relaxing in the witch's presence. She stiffened; she must not give the witch that power.

Afterward, the adults and the boys sat in the living room. Mark took paper and crayons and knelt at the coffee table, drawing, while Alex climbed into the rocking lap. Only Laura was left out, alone in her room with the murmur of voices drifting down the hall.

A long time later she heard the front door open and the sounds of parting. She stepped into the hall to watch, to be certain the witch was really leaving.

"Isn't that sad," Marm remarked when she had closed the door behind the witch.

"What's sad?" Laura asked. She had to know everything about the witch in order to keep them safe. She should not have stayed in her room.

"It explains a lot," Daddy said to Marm, not to Laura.

"Mmmmm," Marm said. "But so sad."

"What's so sad? What explains a lot?" Laura asked.

"Daurice had a brother named Maurice," Mark said. "They were twins like Betsy and Bonnie. When they were little, she set the car on fire and he burned up."

"Oh, Mark!" Marm said, then turned to Laura. "Their mother left them alone in the car, and Daurice played with the car cigarette lighter and dropped it. The car seat caught fire." Before Laura could shrink from the story, Marm continued. "They were only four years old. Daurice managed to open the door on her side and jump out but her brother wasn't able to get out." Marm looked sad. "She's felt responsible ever since."

Laura felt as though she'd swallowed fire. Maurice and Mark. The names even sounded somewhat alike. Like her own and Daurice's. Laura and Daurice.

"What does it explain?" she asked, feeling both light and heavy at the same time. She didn't know whether she was going to float away or sink.

"Well, why she's the way she is," Marm said.

"What way is that?" Laura asked. Was Marm going to admit that Daurice was a witch?

"Strange," Marm said. "It explains why she is strange."

"It explains all of history, Sugarpuss," Daddy said, pulling Laura into a hug. "All of history." But he didn't explain.

Cranberry Beans

Laura lay in bed thinking of Daurice. Had Daurice run around to try to open the car door on her brother's side? Laura imagined it, imagined she was Daurice, opening the car door and leaping free of the flames, then realizing that Mark— Maurice—was not jumping out the other side. She ran around to his side and tugged on the door, but car doors were harder to open from outside than inside, and her hands were so small. Maybe the door was locked. Or the handle was stuck. Or he was just too frightened to think of what to do, and the flames crawled up and nibbled all his clothing and burned him to a crisp, and she was right there watching, screaming, burning her own hands when she touched the hot glass. Why had their

96

mother left them alone in the car? Laura wondered. And how did it all explain Daurice's strangeness?

The thought of Mark in the car with the kidnapper burned her insides. He could have been killed and thrown in the river or buried in some lonely place in the woods. The possibilities branded her with the knowledge that she was just like Daurice. She had been careless about her brother. All along, she had known that saying "All's well that ends well" didn't settle anything. She would grow up to be a witch like Daurice, making candles and walking around the neighborhood looking for rocking chairs, and there was nothing she could do about it.

The next morning, Laura woke with dread. Her dreams had been filled with caldrons and spiders and bats' wings. Then she remembered tomorrow's party and said another thankful. "I'm thankful for the Thanksgiving party," she said softly. Saying the words aloud seemed to diminish the spell that was on her, so she said them again, louder. "I'm thankful for the Thanksgiving party."

She hadn't yet thought of her game, and after her bragging, it would have to be a good one. Perhaps it would take all day and occupy her thoughts.

The door opened. "Well, Laura Cat, you sound as though you're feeling much better," Marm said. "Have a good day. I'm going to the bookshop. Daddy will be here."

"No, wait. Can I go? Do you have any books about games?"

97

"I don't know. We might. But I have to go. You come on down later."

"No, wait. I can dress fast." She slid out of bed, pulled her nightgown off and her shirt and jeans on, and poked her sockless feet into her loafers.

"Socks," Marm said.

Laura scooped up yesterday's pair from where they lay on the floor. "I'll put them on in the car." She didn't know why she was so frantic except perhaps to get out of this house where Daurice had been.

"What about breakfast?"

Laura was already walking down the hall. "I'll eat later. Please?"

They parked on Princess Avenue behind the shop, and Marm opened the store with her own key. To Laura, it was delicious that Marm had a key, almost as if they owned the bookshop, as Zipporah's family owned the clothing store. Laura helped Marm flip on the lights as they walked through the store. She felt a bit proprietary and wondered if Zipporah felt that way when she walked into Greengolds'. And she wondered if Anna ever went to the houses her father built. Important business, she thought, building houses, selling clothes, selling books.

Marm stepped to the sitting area at the front of the shop and plugged in the coffeemaker, then began running eye and hand over bookshelves. Laura flopped down in one of the chairs. It had been Marm's idea to make a spot for people to come sit and have coffee and talk. "Meet me at Queen Street Bookshop" was a motto in Hanover. There were even bumper stickers.

"Card games. Wedding- and baby-shower games. No party games," Marm said, joining Laura and pouring herself a cup of coffee. "Maybe you should go to the library."

"Hmmm," Laura said, remembering what Zipporah had said about the reference librarian. "That's a good idea."

After she'd wandered around the bookstore a bit, she left and crossed to Grand Square. She walked along the sidewalk that circled around the courthouse and came out onto Prince Avenue; then she headed toward the river. The library was part of a riverfront project but was the only thing built so far. Except for the brick-and-glass building and its parking lot, everything else was scrubby. Downriver just a bit she could see one of the seafood-processing plants and the docks where the shrimp boats tied up when they were in port.

In the library she looked around, uncertain about where to go. Except for the times she'd come here with Marm or Daddy, the only place she'd ever gone was into the children's section to the left. She asked for the reference librarian and was directed to the right rear, past adult-sized tables and chairs and the copy machine. There, ahead of her, was a paper and book filled desk with a lettered sign taped to the edge that read REFERENCE DESK.

A man sitting at the desk looked up at Laura's approach. "May I help you?"

"Are you the reference librarian?" Laura asked.

"I am today," he said. "We take turns at the reference desk."

Laura searched his face. Thoughts of hair and pants and Deuteronomy garments and witches whirred in her head. Was this a person, she wondered, who could tell her everything, answer every question even if Marm and Daddy couldn't?

"What may I help you with?" he asked.

"Games," she said quickly, to distract herself from troubled thoughts. Today was not the day, she knew, to tackle all of history. Today she needed to stay busy taking care of today. "I need a really terrific game for a party," she said.

"Well, let's see what we can find," he said, getting up and leading the way to the card catalog. "Do you know how to use this?"

"Yes," she said. She'd been using it since she was seven.

"Well," he said, pulling out the GAM–GEM drawer and thumbing his way toward GAMES. Why had she thought this would be complicated? she wondered. The card catalog was just the same as in the children's department except that there were more cards. He called out the titles of some books and jotted down the names and numbers. "Would you like me to help you find them, or do you think you can find them yourself?"

"I think I can find them," she said. She knew from coming in with Marm and Daddy that if she couldn't reach a shelf there would be a kick stool nearby.

The reference librarian handed her the slip of paper and

100

said, "If you have any problems, let me know."

She wandered toward the tall stacks. If it was hard to find the books, that would be all the better. Witches and spiders were still trying to spin webs in her head.

The number of game books was enormous. She couldn't stop with just the ones he had listed. She collected books from the stacks until she had built herself a fortress of books at one of the adult-sized tables. As soon as she started turning pages she was lost in games. There were simple games and tricky games and stupid games and interesting games and some games that made her laugh just reading about them. The feeling of laughter gave her the same floating feeling as holding her breath or hanging upside-down. She kept sticking her fingers in the pages where there were games that made her laugh, until she ran out of fingers.

Finally, one game made her giggle out loud. Surprised at her own outburst, she looked up and around, but no one had noticed. The game was simple. Even stupid, she admitted. But playing it would be funny. She would need beans, popcorn kernels, and straws. The game was to divide the group into two teams, dump beans and corn on the floor, and have one team suction up beans and the other corn, to be carried by straw to separate collecting dishes.

When she started returning books to the shelves, the reference librarian stopped her. "Did you find what you were looking for?"

"Yes, sir," she said.

"Good. I'm glad," he said. Then he patted the table. "Just

101

leave them here. We'll reshelve them. We like to know what books are being used.''

She skipped all the way back to the bookstore, where Marm said, ''It's about time. I didn't think it would take you all day.''

''It's not even lunchtime yet,'' Laura said. She did not add that taking all day was the whole idea. The terrible load of guilt was still pressing on her head. She told Marm what she needed, and Marm gave her the money.

''Be sure you get dry corn, Laura Cat, not the kind that is pre-oiled.''

The advice didn't mean anything until she stood in front of the popcorn. Then she saw. Pre-oiled is exactly what she would have reached for, because it was the kind they always used. What a mess that would make on the Banners' den floor, she thought. And she noticed something else. Popcorn kernels would be too small for the straws. Someone might suck them through the straw and into the windpipe and choke to death right there at the party. That would be an even worse mess on the Banners' floor. She'd have to see what size the straws were.

Since this was an all-day project, she took her time wandering up and down the aisles instead of reading the signs above them. She found the dried-bean section more quickly than she wanted, right there by the rice and noodles. But the varieties of dried beans made her eyeballs revolve. There were shelves and shelves and shelves of dried beans! She had an unsteady moment, wondering how she could possibly choose among them. She read the names. Kidney beans, baby limas, large limas, small white, yellow-eye, navy, pinto, ham. Not to mention the peas—field, black-eyed, and green split. And then she found her beans. Cranberry beans! What better kind for a Thanksgiving party?

As she picked up the package it sagged and shifted to fit her hand. Cranberry beans! She'd never heard of cranberry beans. She tossed the bag into the air and caught it. When they were finished with the game she would use the beans to make a beanbag. She started to toss the bag again but thought better of it. If the bag split she'd be playing the bean game, solo, right here in the store.

Straws were the hardest to find. She walked up the aisle with soap powder and soap liquid, brooms and mops and pet-food, and down the aisle with canned fruits, vegetables, juices. On the aisle with paper products—towels napkins, plates—she slowed down and stopped. If this were her store, here is where she would put the straws. She looked along the shelves and there they were.

To have choices even with straws surprised her. Should she get the plain or the flexible? The diameter of a straw was $15/64$ inch, the label on the box told her, but what was the diameter of a popcorn kernel? She picked up a package of the plain straws, walked back to the bean shelf, chose black-eyed peas in place of corn for the other team, and marched off to the checkout counter. Having tended to these matters and made

103

these decisions by herself, she felt like Her Highness of Hanover. Fears of becoming a crazy witch had been chased to the back caverns of her mind.

On Saturday afternoon they gathered at Anna's to make decorations.

"I thought we could make Pilgrim collars and Indian headbands and have everyone be a Pilgrim or an Indian," Anna said. She had all colors of paper ready.

"That won't work," Laura said. "Everyone will want to be an Indian." Who would want a drab white collar when they could have a headdress full of colorful paper feathers? Laura wondered.

Anna looked surprised. "I wouldn't want to be an Indian. I'd want to be a Pilgrim."

I should have known, Laura thought. Anyone as unadventurous as Anna would never want to be an Indian. But didn't Anna have enough sense to know how adventurous the Pilgrims must have been to sail an unknown ocean to an unknown place?

"Well, it might work," Laura said, thinking of the teams she needed for her game. "If we make four Pilgrim collars and four Indian headbands, that will be the division for teams."

"What teams?" Zipporah asked. "My game doesn't have teams."

"Neither does mine," said Anna.

"Mine does," Laura said.

"What is your game, Laura Cat?" Anna asked. "You

haven't told your game. Or you, either, Zipporah. Are they secret?''

"Mine's not," Laura said.

"Mine, either," said Zipporah. "In fact, it's a little tricky and I need you two to learn it and help keep things straight."

Laura explained the bean game, and Anna produced two small dishes for the teams to deposit their beans in. Zipporah taught them a game called Rhythm that involved clapping hands, snapping fingers, and calling numbers. It didn't seem much fun to Laura, though Zipporah insisted it would be fun with more people. She hoped her own game wouldn't turn out to be this stupid.

As Zipporah had promised, the Rhythm game was fun. Everyone got confused and missed one time or another, and they played three rounds of it. Tammy was the last one in twice, so she won the prize. In the I'm Going to America game, Laura was an *F*, an *N*, and a *V*. She named flour, needles, and vessels, but on *V* she couldn't name everything back to *A* and she was the first one out. Tammy, with an incredible memory, won that one, too.

During the bean game, cranberry beans got put into the black-eyed-pea container and black-eyed peas got put into the cranberry container, and everyone giggled so much they kept dropping the pea or bean they were trying to carry. The Pilgrims won by having the most of the right kind of bean in their container.

The refreshment table looked wonderful. Mr. Banner had brought some dried cornstalks from a field near where he was working in the country. The girls had placed them on the buffet in an arrangement with squash, pumpkins, and apples. There were pinecone turkeys on the table, one for each guest to take home. And the turkey-shaped cookies went perfectly with the cocoa and marshmallows. Again there was candy corn, which seemed to go as well with Thanksgiving as with Halloween.

When the guests left, the three hostesses hugged one another and danced in a circle.

"This was just as much fun as the Halloween party," Anna said. "We give the best parties."

"We do," said Zipporah.

"Yes, we do," Laura added, wondering whether it was possible to be both a witch and a party-giver.

Hch-hch Hanukkah

As they walked slowly to school, Anna started talking about a Christmas party. Laura knew her friends were walking slowly on purpose to let Mark get ahead. Laura could hardly stand letting the distance grow between her and Mark, but she kept her feet to the pace of her friends and followed him only with her eyes.

"Where shall we have it?" Anna asked.

Zipporah was walking in the middle, and Laura and Anna looked back and forth across Zipporah. They hadn't discussed taking turns, but the first party had been at Laura's and the second at Anna's. Laura dreaded having to have a party at Zipporah's, with GiGi in the house, and she knew

107

Anna was thinking the same thing. When Zipporah didn't jump right in and say, "My house," Laura was hopeful. Maybe Zipporah didn't want to have a party at her house, either, although occasionally she got huffy because they almost never played there. Then Laura and Anna would have to go over and play for a while to soothe Zipporah's hurt feelings.

"Shall we have it at your house?" Anna asked, looking at Zipporah. Laura stared down the street to keep from looking at either of them. Sometimes Anna turned herself into a pretzel, trying to be fair. She herself would have simply let it rest on Zipporah's silence. She was unprepared for Zipporah's angry response.

"You goyim!" Zipporah said, using the word GiGi used so hatefully. She walked away from Laura and Anna and crossed to the traffic island, where Lover's Oak loomed in every direction. Ordinarily Laura would have been right behind, but "goyim," whatever that was, held her to the sidewalk with Anna. Laura and Anna looked at each other and shrugged. They did not say anything to Zipporah at first when they caught up with her and resumed walking.

In a minute, though, Laura said, "Well?"

"Well what?" Zipporah snapped.

"Are you going to tell us what goyim is or not?" Whatever it was, Laura knew it wasn't a good thing to be. GiGi used it when she spouted off in that strange language. Yiddish, Daddy said it was.

"You are," Zipporah said. "You both are."

"I'm not," Anna said. "I'm a Christian."

108

"That's goyim," Zipporah said.

"I'm not a Christian," Laura said.

"Are you Jewish?"

"No."

"That's goyim."

"Well what is goyim? Will you please tell me so I will know what I am?" Mark was out of sight. Laura held her breath a moment, hoping he was across the schoolyard and safely into the school.

"People who aren't Jewish are goyim," Zipporah said.

The school-crossing guard watched them across Princess Avenue, and they started through the schoolyard.

"Well, what does that have to do with whether or not we'll have the Christmas party at your house?" Anna asked.

At the steps, Zipporah moved quickly ahead of them, mounted two steps, and turned to face them. "In the first place, Jews don't celebrate Christmas," she said, looking down on them. Laura was surprised. They didn't celebrate Christmas much at her house, either, and she always felt as if they were the only ones.

"And in the second place, the next holiday is Hanukkah."

Laura kept forgetting there was such a holiday and didn't know anything about it. But because Zipporah was being so forceful, they nodded their heads like obedient students and repeated the word.

"Hanukkah."

"You don't say it with a 'huh,' " Zipporah said. "Pretend you have peanut butter stuck to the roof of your mouth." She made a husky sound in her throat, repeated it several times, then used it for the beginning of the word, "Hanukkah."

"Hch, hch, hch," Laura and Anna said.

"That's really how Haim's name is pronounced but hardly anyone ever says it right. *Hchai*-im."

Laura was amazed. She had noticed but paid no real attention to the scratchy beginning Zipporah always made to Haim's name.

"They are Hebrew words," Zipporah said.

"*Hche*brew?" Laura asked.

Zipporah glared and turned away, preceding Laura and Anna into the building.

"I guess it's not Hchebrew," Laura said. She left Anna and walked by Mark's room to be sure he had arrived safely.

He leaped from behind the door. "I knew you would. I knew you would. Now, you stop following me, Laura Cat."

He startled her so, flooding her with the knowledge that he would report her to their parents, that she walked on down the hall as though she had neither seen nor heard him, as though she just happened to be in the lower hall on some other business.

At lunchtime no one said anything about either Christmas or Hanukkah. But all day long Laura practiced her "hch" so she could talk about it on the way home.

"Tell me about Hanukkah?" Laura asked after school.

Zipporah made a frowny face and didn't even comment on Laura's good pronunciation. With the frown secure on her face

110

she began nodding her head. "I know the names of your holidays and when they are and even a little about them, and you don't even know the names of mine."

"Hanukkah," Laura and Anna said together, with the proper scraping of the roof of the mouth.

"Can we have a Hanukkah party?" Anna asked.

"Tell us about it. We'll never remember anything about it if you don't tell us." Laura said. When Zipporah took ten more steps and still hadn't answered, Laura added, "Well?"

"Well, to tell the truth, we don't usually have a Hanukkah party except at temple," Zipporah said. "It's a family celebration. It's the Festival of Lights."

"The Festival of Lights! Oh, Zipporah, that sounds wonderful," Laura said.

"Well, you said you'd never heard of a Thanksgiving party, either," Anna said, "and that turned out great. Let's have a Hanukkah party. When is it? What are some Hanukkah games?"

Zipporah freed one arm from her books and slapped her head. "I can see it now. Pin the Flame on the Candle."

"Candles?" Laura asked. The thought of candles made her uneasy.

"Candles are the lights part of the Festival of Lights."

"And a celebration is the other part?" Anna said.

"Anna, sometimes you're brilliant," Zipporah said.

"What do you have to eat?" Anna asked.

Laura didn't care about food. She knew already that she

did not want to have a party with candles and GiGi.

"Potato latkes," Zipporah said. "We'll have to make potato latkes."

"What are they?" Anna asked. It sounded to Laura as if both Anna and Zipporah were gearing up for a Hanukkah party.

Zipporah shook her head again. "Part of the party will be to surprise you with what it is all about. And that includes potato latkes."

Laura hoped it would be acceptable to be sick for Hanukkah, if not for Thanksgiving.

At supper Laura announced they might be having a Hanukkah party at Zipporah's. "It's Jewish," she said.

"Do you know what Hanukkah is?" Daddy asked.

"No," Mark said. "What is it? Haim is Jewish."

"It's called the Festival of Lights," she said. She noticed with surprise that Mark said Haim's name with a "hch." "Finding out about it is going to be part of the party, so don't tell us now."

"Am I invited?" Mark asked.

"No," she said.

"Then I want to know now."

"Me, too," said Alex.

Laura thought that she, too, would like to hear about it in the safety of their supper table, rather than in the middle of candles and GiGi at Zipporah's. Instead, she asked a question about something else.

"What I want to know," she asked, "is what holidays do

112

we have? Anna has Christmas and Easter, and Zipporah has Hanukkah.''

"Zipporah also has Passover, Rosh Hashanah, and Yom Kippur," Marm said.

"See? What do we have?''

"We have Halloween, Thanksgiving, New Year's, Valentine's Day, April Fools' Day, May Day, the Fourth of July, and Labor Day," Daddy said. "To name a few.''

"But everyone has those.''

"Laura Cat, people who are not religious are not organized into groups. We celebrate whatever and whenever we want. And we don't celebrate anything we don't want. We celebrate the differences among people.''

"Who else has ice cream and cake for breakfast on birthdays and unbirthdays?'' Marm asked.

"Or dimes in the cake?'' Daddy added.

"Or thirty-one candles till New Year's Day?'' Marm said. In her new distaste for candles, Laura had forgotten their own warm blaze as they lit one more each day from December 1 until December 31. They had begun this celebration only three years ago—this was the fourth—to clear up Laura's confusion about the New Year. She'd gone back to school after the holidays and been sick with disappointment to find she'd been kept back in first grade when she was supposed to go to second grade "next year" and this was the next year. They had Happy New Year gifts instead of Christmas gifts, usually one present each, and they had special surprise unbirthday presents sometimes during the year. Still, this wasn't what Laura

113

meant. These things were not enough. She seemed to need something larger than family to purge the witches, to keep her from growing up to be a witch.

As though he could read her mind and heart, Mark said, "Laura Cat's afraid of witches."

"Oh, she's just pretending," Marm said. "To tease you."

"No," Mark said. "She's afraid of Daurice. She thinks Daurice is a real witch. She thought Daurice was going to eat me for Thanksgiving."

Laura didn't look up. She knew her parents wouldn't like what Mark had just said. But how could she explain?

"Oh? Is that so?" Daddy said. "My Ear, why don't you take Laura Cat into the living room while the boys and I clean up the kitchen?"

Laura was apprehensive. She knew he said "My Ear" to make it sound casual, but she also knew they didn't like the way she felt about Daurice. What would Marm say? Marm would be calm and reasonable and make Laura feel even worse. They didn't know she couldn't help the way she felt.

"Oh, I'll help with the dishes," she said, pushing back from the table and starting to clear her own plate, silverware, and glass.

Daddy reached out from the end of the table and intercepted her. He took the dishes from her, nodded toward the living room, and said, "Go on, Sugarpuss."

Marm led the way, sat at the end of the fuzzy sofa, and patted the spot beside her. Laura sat on the other end and left a space in the middle.

114

"Remember at the Halloween party when one of your friends asked where Daurice had been?"

Laura nodded. Pam's question had been lost in the other conversation about trick-or-treating, and Laura's thoughts about the question had been lost in fear of the real witch. It was best not to ask questions about witches.

"Perhaps we should have told you before, but it's rather difficult for a ten-year-old to understand."

"All of history?" Laura rubbed her fingertips back and forth across the nappy fabric of the sofa, smoothing it down, then roughing it up, then smoothing it down again.

Marm tilted her head to the side. She seemed to be watching Laura's hand. "Well, a lot of history," she said. "Daurice's history, anyway. Do you know what it means when a person is mentally ill?"

Laura gasped. "You mean crazy?" Was Daurice crazy? That was even more scary than if Daurice was a witch.

"Well, yes, that's a word for it, though it is an unkind way to put it. When someone is mentally ill, it is not like having a broken arm you can mend with a cast or pneumonia that can be cured with medicine. We all have chemicals in our bodies, and sometimes they get all mixed up with the way we think and feel about things, and it is, well ''

Alex had already abandoned the dishwashing crew and crept to the edge of the room. He was trying to spin a top on the carpet.

"Alex," Marm said, "move the top to the bare floor and you can get it going—

115

"—like a top going off-balance," Marm continued to Laura. "Our bodies and minds are meant to operate smoothly, like a spinning top. But when something goes wrong with the chemicals, they go out of balance and wobble."

Alex had the top spinning smoothly now, and its separate colors blended in the whirl. Laura felt her chemicals and her thoughts and her feelings whirling, blending, turning her into a crazy or a witch.

"What happened to Maurice was partly Daurice's fault because she played with the cigarette lighter, but she was only four years old. Those children shouldn't have been left alone in the car." Marm held a hand out, fingertips angling into the air. "But things happen."

"Accidents," Laura said.

"Yes. Every one of us is careless sometimes. We drop things, or forget things—"

Like brothers, Laura thought. Like keeping an eye out.

"—or step on someone's toe. And most of the time it doesn't matter much."

All's well that ends well, Laura thought. But it did matter. Everything mattered.

"But sometimes it makes for terrible, horrible, awful tragedy. Like with little Maurice. And even with tragedy—especially with tragedy—we need to be able to forgive ourselves and not grieve forever."

Alex was alternately spinning the top and rolling it back and forth, making tracks on the carpet.

"That's what Daurice has done. Grieve forever. And it has

116

made her strange. She's spent most of her life in a hospital for the mentally ill. But they are releasing people like Daurice who won't hurt anyone, or hurt themselves, and who can take care of themselves. She needs friends and she needs love, just like the rest of us. Do you understand any of this?''

"A little," Laura said. She hoped she would be able to take care of herself. Surely, surely, she could. She'd found the cranberry beans.

"I understand," Alex said.

Marm winked at Laura. "What do you understand, Alex, sweetheart?"

"Daurice is our friend."

Laura felt old. She wished she could be three years old again and have such simple understanding.

"What we have to do when life gets hard is to go easy on ourselves. Daurice was too hard on herself and it made her sick," Marm said. "There's nothing to be afraid of with Daurice. Do you understand?"

"I guess so," Laura said, nodding. She wondered how one went easy on oneself. She wondered how to tell Marm it was herself she was afraid of now, not Daurice. She didn't know how to form her questions.

Laura slid to the floor and scrambled over to Alex.

"Let me," she said. She took the top from him and set it whirring and humming five times faster than he ever could.

Wheelchair Hopscotch

When Anna asked again about the Hanukkah party, Zipporah said, "Well, come to my house to play hopscotch and I'll tell you." Laura knew it was a day they would have to play at Zipporah's to make up for all the times they hadn't.

"Mother said okay to the Hanukkah party, sort of," Zipporah said as she chalked hopscotch squares on the broad walk that led to the door.

"What do you mean, sort of?" asked Anna.

Laura let Anna ask all the questions. She glanced at the wheelchair ramp that also led to the door, and she glanced at the windows to see whether GiGi was peeping out at them. She was afraid she might have to invite "Grandma" to come

118

to the Hanukkah party, too. Was it possible, she wondered, to have cranberry mousse for Hanukkah?

"Well." Zipporah finished sketching squares and put a smooth-edged piece of glass in the number-one square. "She suggested that I just have the two of you and not K, P, RST."

Anna nodded. Laura was not surprised. The Greengolds must not want a bunch of chattering girls to get on GiGi's nerves. Especially goyim. She noticed Anna examining the windows, then seeming to gauge the distance across the street to safety.

"GiGi's not going to come out here and turn you into a Jew."

"Zipporah!" Anna said.

Laura set a nickel in place as her marker. She'd been very lucky with nickels and had learned to throw them so they landed flat and didn't hit the rim and roll away.

"We don't go around trying to change everyone like you do."

"Zipporah!" Anna said again.

"Well, it's the truth, isn't it?"

Without saying a word, Laura declared herself first and hopped over the first square into the second to begin the game. It was the truth, she thought, as she made the two-footed turn in the double squares at the end. Of the various church people who sometimes came to "visit," there had never been anyone Jewish.

"But if you're not a Christian . . ." Anna began, letting her voice trail off.

Laura knew exactly where that trail-off led. She stooped,

picked up her nickel, hopped out, turned, and threw the nickel into the second square. If you weren't a Christian, you would go to hell. Marm and Daddy didn't believe in hell. She hopped over the first two squares and moved one foot, two feet, one foot, two feet to the end turn.

"If you're not a Christian you're not a Christian, and that's all that means," Zipporah said.

Laura was back down the squares, picking up the nickel. She hopped into the second square, then over the first one, threw the nickel into the third square, and began again.

"When are you going to miss?" asked Zipporah.

"Never," Laura said, but as she spoke, the nickel skittered out of the fourth square. It was a sweater day, but the hopping had made Laura hot. She pulled off her sweater and tossed it onto the grass.

"Ha!" Zipporah said and hopped into the game. On the return trip, when Zipporah picked up her marker, the number-one box was empty. "Anna," she said as she stood on one leg, "you haven't put your token in."

Anna produced a small, flattened stone and placed it in the first square. Zipporah hopped over it and began again. She, too, missed her throw to the fourth square, and Anna began. She caught up with them, passed them, and was hopping for the sixth square when the front door opened. Anna stepped on a line.

"You missed!" Zipporah shouted gleefully.

Anna froze on the line she had stepped on, for GiGi had rolled out onto the porch.

"If I had my legs I could still out-hop the three of you," the old woman said. Laura looked at the blanket across GiGi's lap. She had never seen the legs that had been amputated at the shinbone. "I used to be the best hopscotcher in five counties," the old woman said. "The best rope-jumper, too."

Anna began backing down the hopscotch squares.

"Afraid of the poor legless old woman, are you?" Gigi asked, her voice as crackly as her skin. Every word sounded like fussing, even when she said what a good hopscotcher she had been.

Abruptly, GiGi whirled the chair down the ramp and rolled down the sidewalk, speeding right toward them.

Laura leaped onto the grass, beyond her sweater.

Anna screamed and ran, barely checking the street for traffic before she bolted across.

"GiGi, pleeeease stop it," Zipporah said. GiGi began spinning the chair. Zipporah stepped around with it as if in some sort of wild dance. "When she knows someone is afraid of her, she likes to scare them more," Zipporah said to Laura.

GiGi darted toward Laura a couple of times, but Laura's sweater made enough of a barrier. She was as frightened as Anna but was determined not to let any old witch—Daurice or GiGi—know it.

"Okay, let me help you get back inside," Zipporah said when GiGi stopped the circling. Zipporah moved to the back of her great-grandmother's wheelchair, but the old woman put on the brakes and held them.

"I want to play hopscotch," GiGi said in her raspy voice.

Zipporah looked at Laura and shrugged.

"Get away," said GiGi.

Zipporah backed away and stood on the grass next to Laura.

The old woman released the brakes on the wheelchair, took a large black button from her pocket, and dropped it into the first square. Without looking at the girls, she whirled around the first square and straddled the chair wheels over the second, third, and onto the fifth. She didn't touch a line of the fourth square, where Laura's and Zipporah's markers were. She ignored Anna's marker, rolled across the sixth box, and circled in the seventh and eighth. Without a pause, she came back down the course until she was back at the second square. Everywhere but the fourth and first boxes, where markers were, she had crossed lines.

"Pick it up for me, Zipporah," GiGi ordered. Zipporah stepped forward, stooped, picked up the button, and placed it in a crackled hand. GiGi rolled across the first square and out. She turned, tossed the button into the second square, and started again. She didn't miss until the sixth square, when, during her end turn, she rolled over the line of the sixth square.

"Oh, I missed," she cried. "Your turn." She waggled a finger at Laura. "You. Your turn."

Laura did not dare refuse, but she wished she had run away with Anna. She was so nervous she could scarcely hop, and she couldn't throw her coin. On the pitch to box five, the nickel landed edgewise and rolled clear up the walk and hit the step. Zipporah made it to the end and started back before she missed. On her next turn, playing by her wheelchair rules, GiGi finished the course and crackled her pleasure at beating them both.

Only later, safe at home in her own territory, where no one's skin looked like a jigsaw puzzle and no one's voice sounded constantly vexed, did Laura have a glimmer of how remarkable it was for such an old, old person in a wheelchair to play hopscotch.

At dinner, when she told about it, she made it sound like fun.

After what had happened with GiGi, Laura wondered if Anna would even come to the Hanukkah party.

"Of course I'm going. What do you mean?" Anna said when Laura ventured to ask.

"Well, GiGi," Laura said. Her own feelings were mixed. Since telling about the hopscotch and making it seem like fun, she could think of GiGi without fear. But she didn't know how she would do face-to-face with her.

"Well, Laura Cat, Zipporah is our friend," Anna said, as though that settled it. Laura wished Anna had been so thoughtful before she'd opened her mouth about sin. That's what had started everything, it seemed, even her fear of witches.

Zipporah told them to come on the last night. Mrs. Greengold, wanting the parents to understand, had called the Fraziers and the Banners to confirm the invitation.

"What do you mean, the last night?" Laura had asked.

"The Festival of Lights is an eight-day celebration," Zipporah said. "All our holidays begin in the evening. And the last night of Hanukkah is a Saturday this year.''

''Ohhh,'' Laura said.

''We get a present every night,'' Zipporah said.

''Ohhhhh,'' Laura said again. People who celebrated Christmas got lots of presents, and people who celebrated Hanukkah got eight presents. Counting her birthday, unbirthdays, and New Year's, Laura didn't think she got eight presents all year. If Zipporah could know her thoughts, Laura knew Zipporah would say, ''That's greedy.''

''Come at five o'clock,'' Zipporah said. ''We'll get everything ready for dinner before we light the candles, though we'll eat afterward.''

''Dinner?'' asked Anna.

''Yes. Don't eat at home. We're having our first dinner party!''

A Calm, Quiet Party!

On the last night of Hanukkah, Anna called Laura at ten minutes to five.

"Are you coming?"

"Of course I'm coming. I'm about to leave."

"Well, I'll meet you out front," Anna said. "I don't want to go by myself."

Laura walked around the corner and watched while Anna crossed the street to meet her. Candles glowed in all of Daurice's windows.

"Are you scared?" Anna asked.

"A little," Laura said, mostly to make Anna think she had company in fear. Laura wasn't so afraid of GiGi anymore.

125

She was more afraid of the witchery of candles—the candles in Daurice's windows and those which would be lighted soon at the Greengolds'. The Fraziers had been lighting their own candles—they were up to fourteen of the thirty-one for the days in December—and they had a nice glow going, but those were home candles, friendly candles.

Zipporah met them at the door. "This party begins in the kitchen," she said, leading the way. Laura saw Anna looking around warily, fearful of a sneak attack by a wrinkled wheelchair driver. Actually, Laura was interested to see how GiGi would behave.

It was definitely Mrs. Greengold's kitchen, but she set the girls to peeling and cutting potatoes, shredding lettuce, and cutting other vegetables for a salad. Carrying on a running commentary, she told them every step of what she was doing to prepare pieces of chicken for baking.

"Where's GiGi?" Laura asked, as they took turns feeding potatoes to the blender.

"Playing backgammon with Goldy," Mrs. Greengold said.

"Goldy?" Laura asked. Anna was quiet, faithfully cutting vegetables for salad now that the potatoes had been turned to slush.

"Daddy," Zipporah explained.

"Oh," Laura said. She didn't know Mr. Greengold was called Goldy. She was relieved. For a moment she thought GiGi might have a twin, and two of GiGi would be too much.

"Now eggs," Mrs. Greengold said, handing one each to

Anna and Laura. Anna cracked hers expertly, and Laura cracked hers all to pieces.

"Never mind," Mrs. Greengold said. "Just pick out the shell and it'll be fine."

Laura took a fork to remove the shell but could get only the biggest parts. The small bits slid away faster than she could draw them up the sides of the cup.

"Just use your fingers," Mrs. Greengold said. "But don't tell anyone. Especially not those two." She pointed to Anna and Zipporah, and they all laughed.

"Especially not you-know-who," Zipporah said.

The eggshell evaded Laura's fingers almost as easily as it had the fork. "Zipporah," she said, "you only *thought* there was no Hanukkah game. There is one. It's Get the Eggshell Out of the Egg, and I lose."

Just as Mrs. Greengold asked the girls to set the table, GiGi appeared in the doorway between kitchen and hall.

"I'll set," GiGi said, and she wheeled into the kitchen as vigorously as she had rolled onto the front walk. Laura and Anna pressed against the cabinets to keep from being run down.

Laura noticed that Mrs. Greengold repeated everything they did—the potato mix, the salad vegetables—in small portions. "What's that for?" she asked, nodding toward the extra shares.

"Shhh," Zipporah said, putting her finger to her lips, and Laura knew it had something to do with GiGi.

In the dining room GiGi wheeled around and around the table, humming loudly, defiantly. Anna beckoned to Zipporah and backed through the doorway GiGi had first come through. Zipporah followed Anna, and Laura followed Zipporah. Laura held her fingers up so the egg would drip down them instead of off her fingertips and onto the floor.

"What is she humming?" Anna whispered.

"Don't you know it?" Zipporah asked.

"Yes, well, it sounds like, well . . ." Anna stopped.

"Like what?" Zipporah asked. "You can say it, really."

"It sounds like 'Onward, Christian Soldiers,' " Anna said, obviously pained to say the words while she was a guest in a Jewish household.

Zipporah laughed. Then Laura laughed, not knowing quite why except that it was funny to see the crabby Jewish great-grandmother going around and around the table humming a Christian song.

"GiGi grew up next door to a Methodist church," Zipporah said. "She loved the music and learned all the hymns before she knew English. After she learned what they meant, she quit singing the words. She didn't come from England. She came from Yugoslavia." Zipporah winked at Laura. "And I'll bet she brought bagels."

They heard Mr. Greengold come into the kitchen and announce, "Time for menorah," and they scampered back into the kitchen. Laura was going to finish retrieving the eggshells, but the cup was gone.

"I got them," Mrs. Greengold said. "The eggs are in potato latkes now, shells and all."

"Mother, no!"

128

"A joke, Zipporah, a joke. Don't you know a joke when you hear it?"

They filed past GiGi as they went through the dining room to the living room. GiGi hovered in the doorway between the rooms. Haim appeared with the hair-every-which-way affenpinscher at his heels.

"I wondered where Schnitzy was," Anna said.

"With Haim, always with Haim," Zipporah said, as she held up a nine-branched candelabrum.

"That's the menorah," Haim said, and his words ran over those of Zipporah, who was saying the same thing. She glared at him, waited a moment, then repeated her words.

"This is the menorah," she said. "This is the servant candle." She placed it in the middle socket of the menorah. "And these represent the eight days of Hanukkah." She set the colorful candles in place. "The candles are made in Israel."

Haim, Zipporah, and their parents said a prayer and GiGi talked along in the strange language she used.

The dog wandered between Laura and Anna, sniffing them.

"That's right, Schnitzy," GiGi said. "You know there's someone here who doesn't belong."

Zipporah ignored GiGi's remark. "Usually we don't tell the Hanukkah story every night, but since you don't know it, I'll tell it," she said.

"Light the Hanukkah candles," GiGi said from the doorway. "Those who want to hear the Hanukkah story should go to temple."

129

Anna turned pale, as though she might yet be in danger of being run over by the wheelchair.

Mr. Greengold put a hand on Anna's shoulder. "Anna, some households are made up of mother, father, ten-year-old daughter, and two babies. Others are made up of mother, father, daughter, son, and great-grandmother. Do you understand me, Anna?"

"Yes, sir, I think so," Anna muttered. At a signal from her father, Zipporah began the story.

"A long time ago there was war between some of the Jewish people and some people called Syrians. The Syrians defiled the Jewish Temple in Jerusalem and contaminated the supply of oil for the menorah used in the Temple service. The Jews won the war. It was one of the first wars fought for religious freedom—for ideals, not material gain. Afterward, the Jews found one jug of pure oil, enough for only one day.

"But," Zipporah went on, "a miracle happened there. The oil burned for eight days. And in celebration of this miracle, I light the Hanukkah candles." She lit the servant candle with a match and used the servant candle to light the other eight. Laura liked these candles, these Hanukkah candles. They were like large twisted birthday candles, of different colors. They did not remind her at all of witches.

"And here are your Hanukkah gifts," said Mrs. Greengold. She handed a beautifully wrapped present to each of the girls and one to Haim.

"They shouldn't have Hanukkah gifts," GiGi said, and she whirled her chair and sat with her back to them. Anna looked uneasy, and Laura was embarrassed. She shouldn't have a gift. She wasn't Jewish.

"Go on, go on. The children always have a gift," said Mr. Greengold. "It's a small thing, so don't worry yourself. Open it quick and see if it bites."

"Go ahead," said Zipporah. "I'm the hostess. I have to wait for you." Haim had already ripped into his and found a Rubik's Cube. Laura pulled the wrapping loose on hers, and Anna and Zipporah did the same. She knew it wasn't a Rubik's Cube; it was the wrong shape.

"Just what I wanted," Zipporah said, holding up a yellow yo-yo.

"Thank you so much," Laura said. She also had a yo-yo, an orange one.

Zipporah looped the end of the string and slid it onto her finger.

"Not in the house, Zipporah," Mr. Greengold said. "I know you. You'll try around-the-world and crack me in the head."

"Thank you so much," Laura said again. "We've been wanting one, haven't we, Zipporah?"

More quietly, Anna said, "Thank you." Probably, Laura thought, Anna had never wanted a yo-yo.

"Guess who told them we might like one?" Zipporah said. She hugged her parents and started toward GiGi. "A hug for you, too, GiGi," she said. Before Zipporah could reach her, GiGi rolled into the dining room and kept the table between them.

Laura looked nervously at the Greengolds, but Mrs.

Greengold herded Laura and Anna past Zipporah and into the kitchen. Zipporah threw hugs and blew kisses across the table to her great-grandmother. "I love you, GiGi," Zipporah said, and followed the others into the kitchen.

"I'm not allowing you girls near the hot grease," Mrs. Greengold said. "You'll just have to stand back and watch." She put dollops of the potato latke mixture into a frying pan and they flattened out.

"Pancakes?" Anna asked.

"Potato pancakes," Zipporah said. " 'Latkes' means pancakes."

They were served with sour cream and applesauce, which Laura didn't think she would like, but she did. Now that everyone else was in the dining room, GiGi was in the living room eating from a tray. Laura noticed that the old woman was eating the small portions Mrs. Greengold had prepared separately.

"I would like to eat at the table," GiGi said. "This is my house."

Laura kept her eyes on her food.

"You're welcome to come to the table," Mrs. Greengold said. "We would like very much to have you at the table."

"Let *them* eat on trays," GiGi said. "Let everyone go home."

Anna looked miserable.

"Remember the makeup of households, Anna," Mr. Greengold said.

Laura almost laughed. It was certainly not funny, but she suddenly saw herself shouting for Daurice to get out of her house.

"This is your house," Mrs. Greengold said, "but it is also our house and these are our guests."

GiGi commenced the type of ranting and raving Laura had been familiar with since playschool days. Fussing, but in no language she understood.

"I think we should send her to her room," Haim said.

"We don't send great-grandmothers to their rooms," Mrs. Greengold said.

"If I acted like that, you'd send me to my room," Haim said.

"That's true," his father said.

"Then it's not fair," said Haim.

"That is also true," Mr. Greengold said. "It is one of the many unfairnesses of the world. But that's the way life is."

"Now I suggest we just ignore certain behavior and continue with our meal," Mrs. Greengold said. And they did.

The candles were still burning after dinner, but just barely. The girls sat watching the last flickers, not talking, not thinking the party needed any games.

GiGi whirled in and blew out the candles with one huge puff.

"GiGi!" Zipporah said. "That's not nice."

"*That's* not nice," GiGi said, pointing to Anna and Laura. She began turning circles in the living room and wouldn't stop, so Zipporah finally ushered her friends outside.

"I should have warned you about GiGi," Zipporah said, once they were out front.

"We know about GiGi," Laura said. "She's terrified us since we were three."

"Uh-huh," Anna said.

"Mother protected you from her some then," Zipporah said. "This time she said to let you accept us as you found us, GiGi and all." She held her hands out, palms up, as if to say she wasn't sure she agreed with her mother.

"It's okay," Laura said. She saw herself so clearly, saw how she would have acted toward Daurice if she'd been allowed. She was glad she had not been allowed to act that way. And at the same time she had a rush of warm feelings toward the Greengolds because GiGi had been allowed.

"I think you are very brave, Anna," Zipporah said. She let her new toy "yo" down the string but it didn't "yo" back up. "I know you don't like to be scared. You, too, Laura Cat." She rewound the yo-yo by hand.

Laura knew she had not been brave, because she had mostly gotten over being scared before she came. Maybe the Greengolds were brave, having them over in spite of GiGi's protests. And, in her own way, maybe GiGi was brave, too. She hadn't stayed in her room and done without her holiday. She hadn't run over them with the wheelchair, and her words hadn't hurt them.

"As a matter of fact, Zipporah," Laura said, "it was good to have a calm, quiet party for a change!"

134

Going with the Grain

The morning after the Hanukkah party there was a cake and a brightly wrapped gift on the breakfast table.

"Whose birthday?" Alex asked.

"Yeah, whose?" Mark also asked.

Laura knew it was no one's birthday, which meant it was an unbirthday. "Whose unbirthday?" she asked, guessing it was Marm's. Sometimes they were announced ahead, but more often they were surprises.

"It's yours," Daddy said. He started singing "Happy Unbirthday," and everyone joined in. Marm handed her the present.

How unusual, Laura thought, to have presents two days in

a row. Maybe it would never happen again in her whole life. The package was square, but broader and flatter than the box the yo-yo had been in. When she peeled away the wrapping, she found a mounted and framed sand dollar, like some Marm had started making as gifts.

"I got one!" Laura exclaimed. She was the first one in the family to have one. The fabric behind the sand dollar was a scrap of the sofa material instead of the velvet Marm usually used. A tiny inner frown crossed her thoughts. She never had liked that scratchy sofa. Across the bottom her name was spelled out in small wooden letters.

"I want one for my unbirthday," Mark said. "Or for my birthday, whichever is closer."

"It comes with a story," Daddy said.

Laura smiled. Of course. Daddy couldn't do anything without his stories.

"I noticed the way you were rubbing the sofa the other night while we talked," Marm said, "and it gave me an idea. Rub it now, the way you were rubbing it then."

Laura rubbed it, roughing it and smoothing it several times. Apparently this was going to be Marm's story.

"Can you tell which way is right for the cloth?"

"Smooth, of course," she said. She knew this dumb question was leading somewhere. To all of history, probably, she thought. Marm was sometimes as good at all of history as Daddy was.

"That's called going with the grain," Marm said. "The other way is going against the grain. You've been so troubled

136

these past few weeks, ever since Anna made you uncomfortable about wearing pants," Marm said.

Yes, the pants, Laura thought, though those feelings had faded into the distance, what with kidnappings and witches and fears about herself.

"You've been thinking about so many adult sorts of things, I had something I wanted to set you thinking about."

Very carefully, Laura did not change the expression on her face, but her insides fell four inches. Oh, no, she thought. What she wanted was something that would stop her thinking.

"I want you to think about living life with the grain," Marm continued. "Your grain is not like anyone else's. It's just your own, like your fingerprints."

This caught Laura's interest, and her insides settled back into their right places. She had heard that no one in the world had the same fingerprints as anyone else, which was amazing when you thought of all the people there were.

"Really?" she asked. She remembered what Daddy had said about celebrating the differences.

"Really," Marm said. "Sometimes circumstances force you to live against your grain for a while. When that happens, do it as gracefully as possible, but find your own grain again as soon as you can."

Laura rubbed the cloth again. It was easy to tell the grain of the cloth, but how did you tell the grain of yourself?

"As you grow and change, the direction of your grain may change, too. Don't ever be afraid to go with your own grain."

"How will I know it?" she asked.

"I want cake and ice cream," Alex interrupted.

Mark twirled his finger around his ear to indicate that he, too, was bored with the conversation.

Daddy moved to the freezer, removed Laura's favorite fudge ripple, and asked for orders. "Who wants ice cream on cake, and who wants it separate?" The cake, also Laura's favorite, was a yellow butter cake with chocolate frosting.

"When you feel smooth, you're going with the grain," Marm said.

Laura suddenly understood. It was like when her guts had settled a minute ago. That must be what Marm meant by going with the grain.

"Marm doesn't mean things will always be easy," Daddy said, passing the first dish to Laura. "Life can be very hard sometimes, and you can do things that are very hard sometimes but still be with your grain."

Laura smiled and let a bite of ice cream and cake dissolve slowly in her mouth. Even though it was Marm's story, Daddy still had to add to it. But she really understood what he meant. Like going to Zipporah's for hopscotch and Hanukkah. Like being friends with Anna even though Anna thought wearing pants was sinful. Like being polite to her parents' guests even if she didn't like them and she was afraid. When she thought about growing up to be a witch or crazy, the idea went totally against her grain.

"Mmmm," Mark said. "This is just what a boy needs to get his day off to a good start." Just like a comedian, he waited for their laughter. Laura rubbed the fabric against her cheek and felt it go from rough to smooth.

"Laura Cat," said Alex, sticking out a tongue to lick his dish, "I'm glad today is your unbirthday."

"Well," Anna said, "now is Christmas the next holiday? Now can we have a Christmas party?"

"Of course," Zipporah said. "Why don't we have a caroloing party. Between GiGi and the radio, I know all the songs."

Anna said, "Your house, Laura Cat?"

When Laura asked her mother, Marm said, "You girls are certainly having a lot of parties."

"We can't help it if there are so many holidays right together," Laura said. Her mind ran ahead to New Year's, Valentine's Day, St. Patrick's Day, Easter, May Day, the Fourth of July. She knew now that they were all hers if she wanted them to be. "Except for now it will really be only once a month, so just once every three months at our house."

This time they sent out invitations.

> WHAT? A caroling party.
> WHERE? Laura Cat Frazier's.
> WHEN? The Saturday before Christmas.
> PLEASE COME!
> P.S. Also, please practice up.

"Since we will be the leaders, maybe the three of us should practice up," Anna suggested. Laura and Zipporah agreed.

As they began with "Deck the Halls," Zipporah sang out boldly.

"Hey, I can barely hear you," she said to the other two, who were singing weakly. "Come on! I'm singing *your* songs!" She roused them like a cheerleader until they were singing with gusto.

Daddy walked in with a surprised look on his face. "That really sounds very good," he said. "You sound like six people singing."

On the next song, Laura and Anna were singing quietly again.

"What happened?" Zipporah asked.

Anna ducked her head and looked at Laura's father.

Zipporah put her hands on her hips. "If you can't sing for Mr. Frazier, who do you think you can sing for?"

"Maybe we should really go caroling, just us, to get used to it," Anna said. "I think I'm going to be scared."

"Uh-oh," Zipporah said.

"Just on this block," Laura said.

They grabbed their sweaters and started out of the house. This time of year, the weather could be cold enough for coats or warm enough for bare arms. Laura liked the sweater weather.

"Where to?" Zipporah asked.

"To the Martins'," Laura said, indicating the house two doors down. She knew they were Christians and might appreciate the caroling.

The girls huddled together at the bottom of the three steps

to the Martins' small concrete porch. Anna giggled, and she and Laura were unable to get their voices going. Even Zipporah sang weakly.

"Come on, now," Zipporah said.

"They can't hear us with the windows closed and if the television is on," Anna said.

"Good," said Laura. She liked the idea of caroling but wasn't sure she could do it.

"I'll go ring the bell," Zipporah said. "And you be ready. As soon as they open the door, we'll start singing." She stepped up the three steps and looked back at Laura and Anna. "You'd better sing," she said.

"We will," said Laura.

"We really will," Anna added.

Zipporah rang the bell, and even from the bottom of the stairs Laura could feel the vibrations of footsteps coming from within the house. Anna glanced at Laura, stepped onto the grass, and ran. As though attached to Anna with a tether, Laura ran, too. Their steps made no sounds as they fleetfooted it across the grass. They ducked into the azalea hedge and stifled their giggles.

Only then did Laura realize that there were just the two of them huddling in the azaleas. Zipporah was still on the porch, and Mr. Martin was opening the door.

Laura watched a triangle of light fall across Zipporah, and Zipporah sang loudly, "Jingle bells, jingle bells, jingle—" When there were no voices added to her own, Zipporah turned to glare at her friends. Still open with singing, her mouth remained open but changed shape. She looked back at Mr. Martin, standing tall in the door-framed light, then back at the empty spaces where her friends had been.

In the few seconds it took for all this to happen, Laura was filled with remorse. She knew exactly how she would feel if she had been left standing there. Just as she made a move to rejoin Zipporah, Zipporah leaped from the porch and ran toward the Fraziers'. Laura ran after her.

"I'll kill you!" Zipporah said when she saw Laura. "I'll kill you!" Zipporah reached the door first and ran inside. "Do you know what they did to me?" she wailed to Laura's parents. She repeated the question like a stuck record and could not get past it.

Laura and Anna, stricken with guilt, collapsed—laughing—onto the sofa.

"I'm sorry," Laura said immediately. "I don't mean to be laughing." She covered her mouth to hold back the mirth, but it would not be contained.

"You looked so funny standing there by yourself," Anna crowed.

"I'll funny you," Zipporah said.

"Tell me what they did to you," Marm said.

Zipporah told, and during the telling, Laura and Anna managed to quell their laughter and wipe the tears from the corners of their eyes.

"I'll funny you," Zipporah repeated when she had finished telling what had happened. "This is one party you'll give without me."

142

"Oh, no, Zipporah!" Anna cried. "No! No!"

Laura added her own "No! No!" though she noticed Zipporah was not edging toward the door. After seventeen apologies and forty-two promises, Zipporah was mollified enough to agree to be one of the carolers.

Laura Right-Side Up

By the night of the party, the weather had turned quite cold. Gloved and muffled, the caroling party set out for the Martins'.

"This makes me feel just like the pictures of carolers," Anna said, cuddling into her scarf. "All wrapped up."

"All wrapped up and *singing*," Zipporah said.

"I'll sing, Zipporah. I really will," Anna said.

"Did I tell you what they did to me?" Zipporah asked the others. She hadn't, so she did. "I'll sing, but I won't ring any doorbells."

This time, Laura mounted the stairs. When she rang the bell she stood sideways so she would know if there was a

144

retreat. Mr. Martin opened the door, and the girls all stood steady and sang with spirit.

"What happened the last time?" he asked when they were done.

The question triggered Laura's and Anna's funnybones, and this time Zipporah laughed, too. She pointed to the two deserters. "They ran off and left me."

"Well, I want Mrs. Martin to hear you. Will you wait? You won't run away, will you?" Mr. Martin disappeared, then reappeared with his wife, and they sang again.

"Lovely, lovely," Mrs. Martin said. "Thank you so much. And just a minute. I want to give you something."

This was the time to run away, Laura thought. What was Mrs. Martin going to give them? This wasn't Halloween. This wasn't trick or treat. They hadn't come to sing so they could get something.

But Mr. Martin was still in the doorway, holding them with his eyes and his conversation. Mrs. Martin came back and handed each of them an orange. With surprise, appreciation, and embarrassment, they thanked the Martins. Then they ran back to Laura's and put the oranges on the porch and started out again.

The more doors they knocked on and the more they sang, the louder and happier they sang. Some people gave them little gifts—oranges, apples, candy canes, nuts—and some gave only thanks. But everyone liked the caroling and the carolers.

In their progression from house to house, they came to the Larges'. Laura glanced up at the ever-present candles burning in the second-floor windows. They sang for Mrs. Large, and Laura hoped they would continue along at ground level. She forgot that everyone here had been up those stairs.

No one even asked the question "Shall we go upstairs?" When they pocketed the candy canes Mrs. Large had given them, six of the eight moved in a herd to the side of the house.

"Oh, come on," Zipporah said when she noticed the two laggards. "She's just like GiGi. She doesn't mean any harm."

Laura wasn't sure GiGi meant no harm, but at least she hadn't done any. She and Anna followed at a distance. When they reached the corner of the house, Anna stopped.

"This is as far as I'm going," Anna said.

Laura looked at her. Anna was hesitant, reluctant, and unadventurous. Laura did not like to show her fear. And even as she stood there she realized she wasn't really afraid of Daurice anymore. She had been afraid for outside reasons at first—because Daurice was so strange, sitting in the chair and rocking, rocking. Then she'd been afraid for inside reasons—because she feared she might grow up to be like that.

Somewhere underneath her reluctance, there was the smoothness of going with her grain. She moved toward the others, and after she had placed a foot on the first step, her legs took her on up automatically.

The witch opened the door before the bell rung. Laura thought they must have sounded like a flock of turkeys climbing the stairs. The girls sang out immediately, and Daurice's smile shimmered in the candle glow.

When the singers stopped for breath at the end of one carol,

Daurice looked over the heads of six girls to Laura. "Laura Cat, thanks for bringing your friends to sing." Laura almost cringed at being singled out, but the others turned and looked at her with favor. Daurice turned away from the doorway, and when she turned back, she gave each of them a sweet-smelling, short, stubby candle.

Amidst the oohs and ahs of acceptance, she said, "Can you do this?" Stepping back into the apartment, she made some hand movements above a candle—the same mysterious movements Laura had observed from the sidewalk a few weeks ago.

The girls crowded up to the door. Laura found herself crowding, too, saying, "Let me see. Let me see." Hands together and thumbs up, Daurice was opening and closing her little fingers against her ring fingers. When Laura wiggled to the front, she saw the shadow of a barking dog on the wall of the apartment. Then there was a rabbit. Then an old man. Amidst the expressions of delight from the girls, Daurice was making shadow pictures.

"I can sing Christmas carols, too," Daurice said, looking directly at Laura. "Could I go with you?"

It was too much for Laura. She didn't know what she was doing up here, anyway.

"Of course." Zipporah had already answered. As though she had planned for it, Daurice had her coat, hat, and scarf right by the door. Almost before Laura knew what was happening, Daurice was on the porch and Zipporah had taken her hand and was leading her down the stairs.

147

Laura shrank back and plastered herself to the railing as she had plastered herself to the cabinets at the Greengolds' when GiGi had come blustering through the kitchen.

Laura heard Zipporah's voice saying in her head, "She's just like GiGi." Laura felt her grain, loosened herself, and scrambled down the stairs, weaving her way to the front of the group. At the bottom, she darted ahead, came alongside Daurice, and took hold of her other hand.

"Me, too," said Susan, taking Laura's hand. Other "me, too's" followed as the remaining girls all joined hands. Now that she was three times removed from Daurice, even Anna latched on. The three girls and their party friends snake-chained toward the sidewalk.